Crime in Kensington

CHRISTOPHER ST JOHN SPRIGG

 Moonstone Press

This edition published in 2019 by Moonstone Press
www.moonstonepress.co.uk

Originally published in 1933 by Eldon Press Ltd

Introduction copyright © 2019 Moonstone Press

ISBN: 978 1 8990 0004 3

A CIP catalogue record for this book is available from the British Library

Text designed and typeset by Tetragon, London
Cover illustration by Chrissie Winter and Charlie Fischer
Printed and bound by in Great Britain by TJ International, Padstow, Cornwall

Contents

Introduction

Crime in Kensington, originally published in 1933 by Eldon Press, was the first detective novel by Christopher St John Sprigg. The book introduces amateur sleuth Charles Venables and is set in a residential hotel full of eccentric characters with dubious and possibly murderous motives. Although it was his first venture in the genre, Sprigg was already an experienced writer of short stories and *Crime in Kensington* combined an intricate plot with an appealing sense of humour and ironic tone. ("Viola had two passions in life, her art and her bridge. Charles had hoped to be a third, but he was beginning to abandon hope. He felt that while he might make her a satisfactory partner in life, he would certainly let her down at bridge.") Charles Venables is a journalist, and when his proprietress disappears and the police come up empty-handed, he must put his investigative skills to work.

Sprigg was born in October 1907 in Putney to a literate family of writers, journalists and editors. His father was a biographer and editor of various periodicals, including the *Daily Express*; his grandfather had worked on newspapers in Ireland and Scotland before becoming editor of the *Nottingham Guardian*; his grandmother wrote a column, "House and Home", for the *Daily Mail* for over twenty years. The youngest of three children, Sprigg was sent to Catholic boarding school quite young—just shy of his fifth birthday—possibly due to his mother's deteriorating health. She died when he was eight and Sprigg continued to board until a downturn in family finances prompted a departure from schooling at age fifteen.

Sprigg then became a trainee reporter at the *Yorkshire Observer*, where his father was currently literary editor, and father and son lodged together in a boarding house in Bradford. He kept wry observations about the residents, such as "two old ladies in the boarding house who used to put on their hats, gloves & prayer books to listen to the BBC Church Service in their room on Sundays and who used to send invitations by the maid to the next door bedroom inviting them to teas". No doubt these experiences provided background for *Crime in Kensington*, with its genteel Garden Hotel and comic residents Miss Geranium, who receives messages from the prophet Ezekiel, and Miss Mumby, owner of the "tracker" cat Socrates.

After two years of this apprenticeship Sprigg returned to London. With the advent of aeroplanes and flying had come magazines that catered to those interests. In February 1925, older brother Theo became editor of *Airways* magazine and Sprigg his deputy. Over the next eight years they contributed articles aligned with their interests, Theo dealing with people and travel and Sprigg with science, engineering and book reviews. It was an era in which great strides were being made in aeronautics—new speed records, new technology and new routes. *Airways* targeted the non-technical public interested in air travel. In 1928 the magazine even acquired its own aeroplane.

During this time Sprigg also produced technical books, such as *The Airship, Its Design, History, Operation and Future*, and air adventures stories for *Popular Flying* magazine. He had a fondness for noms de plumes, writing adventure stores under the names "Arthur Cave" and "Icarus", using "St John Lewis" for articles in *Airways* and "Christopher Beaumont" for his book reviews. For his later non-fiction work, Sprigg used his mother's maiden name, writing as Christopher Caudwell.

*

Crime in Kensington was followed by a second Charles Venables story, *Fatality in Fleet Street*, later that year. Around this time a slump in advertising revenue saw *Airways* magazine decline and it eventually folded in 1935. The lack of a steady wage increased Sprigg's output; he produced thirty aviation articles and six short stories in 1934, as well as two detective novels, *The Perfect Alibi* and *Death of an Airman*. The final outing of detective Charles Venables, *Death of a Queen*, appeared the following year as well as another thriller, *The Corpse with the Sunburnt Face*. Both books reflected Sprigg's growing interest in anthropology: the first deals with matrilineal succession in an imaginary country in Eastern Europe; the second is set partly in West Africa.

In 1935 Sprigg largely abandoned detective literature to pursue a project that combined his interest in science with his lifelong love of poetry. Total conversion to Marxism added a third strand that Sprigg applied to this endeavour, which would be published posthumously as *Illusion and Reality*. He joined the Communist Party and in letters to friends shared plans to go to Moscow and his efforts to learn Russian ("The language isn't too bad, but the alphabet is fairly bloody.")

The Spanish Civil War broke out in July 1936; the dormant hostility between Fascism and Communism ignited and Spain became a symbol of that ideological struggle. The pressure to "do something" became intense among the young and idealistic, and the local communist party was instrumental in forming the British Battalion of the International Brigade. Determined to help, Sprigg fundraised for an ambulance, which he drove through France and delivered to the loyalists. Friends and family tried to dissuade him, arguing that his literary gifts and publications under development were best served by staying at home. However, Sprigg remained committed, believing the Spanish war to be far more than a national conflict, and that its outcome would determine the future of civilization in

Europe. On arrival in Spain he joined the Brigade troops at Albacete. After four weeks of training and poorly armed—the Brigade was equipped with left-over and out-of-date weaponry no one else wanted—his unit was thrown into the Battle of the Jarama River in February 1937. Sprigg was killed in the first day of fighting along with more than half of his battalion.

Until recently Christopher St John Sprigg was largely remembered for his Marxist writing and poetry, all of which were published posthumously under the name Christopher Caudwell. The republication of *Death of an Airman* by the British Library in 2015 has helped revive interest in his detective fiction. Copies of *Crime in Kensington*, published in New York around the same time under the name *Pass the Body*, have been exceedingly rare. This Moonstone Press edition of the first Charles Venables novel gives crime fiction readers an opportunity to enjoy Sprigg's lively and well-crafted work.

Chapter One

SOME SINISTER ENCOUNTERS

Charles Venables was walking slowly through the westerly and more unfashionable purlieus of Kensington. His subsequent adventures, remarkable though they were, are not in any way put forward as extenuating this action.

As he strolled along the stucco vista of Tunbridge Gardens, he pulled out a letter from his pocket to verify the address of the place for which he was looking.

> "The Garden Hotel,
> "Tunbridge Gardens,
> "London, W.

"My dear Charles,—How terribly amusing! The idea of you as a gossip-writer—sorry, society journalist—is *distinctly* funny. However, I imagine you will do it rather well, and you were certainly wasting your talents in the exclusively rural pursuits of Tankards. Now that you are coming to live in London you must *definitely* stay at this place for a time, until you can look round and find digs of your own. For one thing, you will amuse me—commercial art is perfectly utter at the moment—and for another, it is comfortable (good plain food, you know) and amazingly cheap. There is something rather *weird* about the place that I cannot *quite* make out yet, but nothing to complain of—rather *intriguing*, in fact. Such *odd* people. Anyway, I am expecting you *directly* you get to London.

> "Ever thine,
> "Viola."

Venables fished up his monocle from the end of its lanyard and through it scrutinized the letter again. Then he looked up. Like so many other residential hotels in Kensington, the Garden Hotel was an uninspiring arrangement of stucco, tiled doorsteps, aspidistras, revolving doors, verandahs and hall porter.

"It looks neither odd nor comfortable," reflected Venables, negotiating the steps, the hall porter, the doors and the aspidistras.

He asked for the manager. Viola characteristically had mentioned no names. "The manager" was a proprietress, Mrs Budge. Venables was conducted into a secluded suite at the top of the building by an alert maid. She left him in the sitting-room, knocked on another door and went through. Scraps of conversation floated back to Venables.

"Someone to see you about living here, a Mr Venables. Friend of Lady Viola."

"I'm too busy," snapped a woman's voice. "Tell him to go away."

"Don't be a fool, Louisa," said a man's voice. "A residential hotel doesn't turn away guests because the proprietress is too busy. Ask Mr Venables to wait, Brown, and say Mrs Budge will not be a moment."

Brown appeared again, gave the message more politely, and went out. Venables was somewhat intrigued by the Garden Hotel's attitude to visitors. He had an intelligent curiosity, and its gratification was not interrupted by scruples against listening at doors and looking at other people's letters lying round. He ambled towards the door and earnestly studied a Japanese print hanging near it. Meanwhile he listened carefully. He could hear the words of a conversation between Mrs Budge and the man distinctly.

"How many times have I told you that we must appear to run this hotel as a commercial proposition?" said the man emphatically.

"All right; all right," replied Mrs Budge. "Anyone would think it was *your* idea the way you carry on."

The remark appeared to infuriate the man. His voice was lowered, but the tone was sufficiently menacing. "Your idea! What's the good of the idea without the brains to carry it out, tell me that. I'm the brains behind this concern, and don't you forget it. My God, if you do, and try to do me down, I'll slit your throat from ear to ear."

Venables had never heard a threat given with more sincerity. The same aspect seemed to strike Mrs Budge, for her reply was the reply of a frightened woman.

"Now then, Georgie, I've never denied it, have I? I've always said you have been wonderful over the whole scheme."

"Well, as I told you before, Louisa, that's not enough. I'm not sufficiently covered, as things are at present, and that's a fact. You've put it off and put it off too long. This evening you must write to your lawyers and see that I'm properly taken care of in case you die, and it's no good your saying you're a fine healthy woman. We are all mortal, and one day you may push things too far and get a clout over the head from one of your guests which will finish you."

"Don't say that, Georgie," whined Mrs Budge. "You know I never push things too far with any of them. Small profits, quick returns has always been our motto. They're all cowards, anyway. But I'll see the lawyers look after you all right, and I've never refused to sign any cheque you asked me, have I?"

Venables felt that the conversation was coming to an end, and that it might cause mutual embarrassment if he were found in the suite. He slipped out of the sitting-room and took up his stand in the corridor, hat and stick in hand and with the air of a man who had waited on his feet for a long, long time.

His anticipation had been correct. In a few moments Mrs Budge came out, followed by her interlocutor. "Presumably Mr Budge," thought Charles.

He found it rather difficult to believe that the couple he now saw were really responsible for the conversation he had just heard. Mrs

Budge was *petite*, genial, and dressed in a severe but modern dress with perhaps a surplusage of black beads. A certain insouciance in make-up betrayed the proprietress rather than the manageress. About forty, thought Venables, after speaking to her for a few minutes, efficient, perfect manner. Now what on earth…?

Mr Budge looked strikingly incapable of slitting anyone's throat. Dressed in shiny black, with a wandering grey moustache and grave eyes, he looked somewhat like a Nonconformist lay reader. He glanced keenly at Venables and walked away.

Beneath the normal manner of a proprietress answering the inquiries of a would-be resident, Venables detected a searching scrutiny which was not the less keen for being veiled. He responded to it almost automatically, with a slight emphasis of his stutter and sufficient monocle-play to produce the required impression of vacuity.

Mrs Budge saw a reasonably good-looking young man of about twenty-nine, with a colourless expression, and clothes, if anything, a little too well cut. Shoes and hair highly polished; natty handkerchief in breast pocket; spotless gloves; a friend of Lady Viola Merritt. Apparently she was satisfied, for Venables felt the scrutiny turned off like a tap.

They were looking round a suite, well furnished with plain, unpolished wood, no pictures, and an air of distinction foreign to a Kensington residential hotel.

"I'm a sneak-guest," prattled Venables. "No relation to a sneak-thief, so you need not worry about the spoons. I put the bits in the *Daily Mercury* saying how charming Lady Blossom looked, who is, of course, the daughter of the Earl of Loamshire. A harmless profession, if somewhat monotonous."

Mrs Budge appeared satisfied, and they discussed terms. Venables was frankly surprised. The Garden Hotel was a comfortable-looking place, and the staff, furnishing, and probably the food was good. The price was much too low. Decidedly the oddest thing about the place.

II

Charles was going down to dinner when he met on the stairs a queer little foreigner, obviously Oriental. He was comparatively young, but a battered glass eye and a small moustache asymmetrically mounted on a thick upper lip contrived to give him a sinister expression. He leered at Charles with what the latter rightly assumed to be a cordial look, but which was somewhat more sinister than his normal expression. Then suddenly he gave a start of recognition. He placed one finger against his nose and winked his good eye.

"So our little hostess's game is up," he said, evidently feeling that Charles would appreciate the purport of his remark.

Charles stared.

"Oh, sorry, sorry," apologized the other, effusively, his throaty accent still more pronounced. (Egyptian, thought Charles.) "Not supposed to know, eh? Well, well. You can rely on my not giving you away, what?"

"Do I understand you know me," said Charles, edging away a little apprehensively.

"Your name—no! Your face, yes!" the man replied. "Still you wish to pull wool over our eyes, well, what?" He exploded in a cryptic sequence of explanatory gestures.

"You seem to be labouring under some mistake," Charles answered kindly but firmly. "I'm afraid I don't know you—"

"Of course not, ha ha, what?" the Oriental remarked. Charles came to the conclusion that the frequently repeated "what?" was merely rhetorical. "I hope very much you not know me, but I know you."

"Well then, you have the advantage of me," answered Charles, "with which words our heroine walked away, leaving Jasper biting his lips, speechless."

"What?" the Egyptian said, and though this time Charles Venables opined that the "what?" was meant interrogatively, he did not answer him. He slipped past the fellow and hurried downstairs.

"This is really too awful," Charles remarked to himself. "When one hears a bloke threaten to kill his wife and then immediately afterwards meets a sinister and mysterious Oriental, it is time to move somewhere else, for one has obviously walked into the plot of a thriller of the vulgarest and most exciting description."

III

"Well, Charles," said Viola, as they sat in the lounge in the evening. "What do you think of this place?"

"Fishy, my girl, fishy," replied Charles. "I arrived in time to prevent Budge murdering his wife."

"Good God, Charles, no!" said Viola, startled. "Are you serious? What on earth was happening? Tell me from the beginning."

"You forget I am a journalist now. A small copper coin will purchase to-morrow's *Mercury*, when you can learn the worst."

"Don't be irritating, Charles. Did anything exciting happen? I don't suppose it did. There is something queer about this place, all the same. Look at Mrs Salterton-Deeley, over by the door."

Charles looked. Her hair was of the dyed-in-the-wool flaming red colour, at the sight of which Charles instinctively crossed his fingers. Her eye looked as if it should rove, but it was not roving now.

"She's been crying," said Viola with finality. "I ran into her once before when she was actually weeping. Somewhat awkward. Each time it has happened after an interview with Mrs Budge when she has been quite cheerful before."

"Well, what's extraordinary about that? I have staggered out of hotel managers' offices absolutely broken up. There have been times when cashiers' refusals to cash my cheques have been phrased in language so abrupt and insolent that I have only refrained with an effort from a burst of unmanly tears."

"You will never get on in life unless you drop your deplorable habit of flippancy," said Viola severely. "There are mysterious things about this place. Even if you think nothing of the Salterton-Deeley incident, look at the other guests. They are all absolutely gaga."

Charles looked round with a certain amount of alarm. "Who is the gaunt lady, with the tightly rolled-back grey hair, and surrounded by cats?" he asked.

"Oh, that's Miss Mumby. She's terribly rich, but she spends all her money on séances and cats. I went into her sitting-room once and the whole place was absolutely covered with cats' hairs, and there was some form of cat on every piece of furniture! How the Budges stand for it, I don't know!"

"And who is the lady with the moustache and the mountainous contours?"

"That's Miss Hectoring," answered Viola. "I don't think I've ever heard her utter more than two words since I've been here. She's really a sort of guardian companion to Miss Geranium, who wasn't at dinner."

Tall, stout, and with the glittering black eye and dominant nose of the Highland female, Miss Hectoring stared at the other occupants of the lounge, daring them to invade the privacy which, like a banner, she flaunted in their faces. "A worthless, gangling pack," her expression seemed to say. Women with the same disdain for their company, but with more sensitive skins, would have kept out of the most public of the hotel's common rooms. But that, evidently, was not Miss Hectoring's way. She preferred to be in the midst of them, proof-armoured with contempt, and if she could not create respect, she could make a desert around her.

"Well, what do you think of our menagerie?" asked a clear voice. It was the voice of youth, but the owner, whose name Charles learned in the subsequent introduction, was Miss Sanctuary, looked over sixty, with the wrinkled skin but calm eyes of serene old age. She sat down beside them and produced some knitting from an enormous work-bag. As she bent over the flying needles, with her pure white hair neatly tucked into a bun at the back of her head, she looked like one of those old mothers who wait interminably in the twilight of Hollywood for errant sons and daughters. But Charles detected in her eye a gleam of kindly irony which told him that her attitude of mild benevolence was not altogether disingenuous, that she had that union of a kind heart with a sharp tongue which is not uncommon in the spinster of too certain years.

"What are you doing here, young man?" she went on. "You're a friend of Lady Viola's, I suppose?"

Charles acknowledged it.

"Well, take my advice," she said, "take her away from here! It's unhealthy living with this crowd of old derelicts. I see the humour of being one myself, and I get a certain amount of amusement out of watching people like Miss Mumby; but it's quite wrong for Lady Viola. Take her away!"

"Alas, Miss Sanctuary, the modern girl cannot be fetched and carried in the good old Victorian way. I may say that I have offered Viola a good home and a husband, who, although poor and indifferent honest, had a good heart. That was in the rural glades of Tankards, and I was told by the object of my affections that she would wait till we were both earning our livings, and further, that she would be prepared to bet that she was earning her living before I was." He paused. "She was right!"

"Shut up, Charles," said Viola, the equivalent of the Victorian maiden's blush.

Miss Sanctuary looked at her keenly.

"Well, I should persevere," she said to Charles.

"I think I shall stay here for a little, at any rate," Charles remarked suddenly.

Viola followed his eyes. "That's Mrs Walton who's just come in," she answered. "She is lovely, isn't she?"

"Divine," declared Charles emphatically. "She looks exactly like those shepherdesses and nymphs that Greuze paints. I never thought them possible before, and I certainly never expected to see one in modern clothes."

"I wish someone would take her away, too," sighed Miss Sanctuary. "She's a widow, I believe, but I can't imagine that she will remain one long unless she wants to. By the way, have you heard about Mrs Budge?"

They hadn't.

"She's ill in bed—with pleurisy, the doctor thinks. It was very sudden. She thought she had a bad cold this morning. Then she got a temperature, and now she's completely laid out. I shall go and sit with her a little, I think, and leave you two. You probably want to talk."

IV

Charles had not seen Viola for three years. He was making up for it now. With her short black hair framing the blameless oval of a perfect complexion, she was worth looking at. The two had been brought up more or less together, for Venables senior had been an old friend and neighbour of her father, the Earl of Buxley. Both their parents had shared in the post-war economic pinch, and Viola was now successfully earning her living as a commercial artist, with a flourishing little studio off Fleet Street. Slade School, Rome Scholarships, and similar fripperies had gone by the board as the economic gale blew harder, and Viola confessed to herself in confidential moments that she made more and better use of her single talent by exposing it in the market-places of Fleet Street than if she had wrapped it in a napkin and taken it to Chelsea. So Viola had been earning a living while Charles was still wandering about the world, fresh from Oxford, and undecided as to what profession would be honoured with his services.

Viola had two passions in life, her art and her bridge. Charles had hoped to be a third, but he was beginning to abandon hope. He felt that while he might make her a satisfactory partner in life, he would certainly let her down at bridge, and Viola appeared to agree.

None the less Viola charmed him as much as ever. Her tidy brain and efficient manner which in so many girls become gritty, thought Charles, and irritate one like breadcrumbs in the bed, gave her classic and clear-cut features a piquancy, as if the Venus de Milo should, in spite of her appearance, prove to be intelligent.

The smoke from his cigar rose perpendicularly, and the coffee was really excellent…

"I made a fatal mistake in coming here," he said gravely. "First of all, the sinister conversation of the Budges, then the sinister encounter on the stairs, and now, most sinister of all, the love interest. If you are really serious about not marrying me, which I find difficult to believe, I can only advise you to leave the place at once…"

V

The Rev. Septimus Blood was surprised. "A Coptic rite," he pressed; "have the Egyptians got a rite of their own?"

"Oh, yes," answered Eppoliki, the little Egyptian medical student. "The oldest rite in Christendom, what?"

The Rev. Septimus Blood was justifiably irritated. Last spring he had given up the Latin rite in favour of the rite of Sarum, and this in turn he had abandoned for the Mozarabic rite, with its Eastern influences. Now these Egyptians apparently had an even older rite.

"Tell me about the vestments," asked Blood. "Is the cope worn for ordinary low mass?"

"Yes, cope and tall hat," answered the Egyptian. "Very impressive indeed, and two thurifers." He was drawing somewhat lavishly and inaccurately on his childhood memories, but he said enough to inflame Blood's curiosity.

"I must learn more of this," said Blood. Short, dark, and with the faint sing-song of a Welsh accent, he was by profession a bacteriologist and a very expert one. On the day he had been ordained, he had become an Anglo-Catholic of such extreme views that any hope of becoming an incumbent of even the most tolerant parish was out of the question, even if he had been prepared to sacrifice the more lucrative profession in which he had carved a niche for himself. He was, however, an unpaid curate at a little church in Houndsditch which the Bishop had given up in despair, and his introduction of the Mozarabic rite had been the cause of much local pride. This Coptic rite sounded distinctly interesting. The tall hat was particularly good. Blood realized that his shortness was a handicap when it came to making an impressive figure on the altar. A tall hat now...

Eppoliki changed the subject abruptly. "The police are on track of this place," he said.

The Rev. Septimus Blood turned pale. "H-how do you know?" he quavered.

"Saw familiar face on the stairs," Eppoliki answered cheerfully. "May be mistaken, of course, what?"

"Good God, I wonder what I ought to do," exclaimed Blood anxiously.

"If you turn round now carefully you will see the detective," remarked Eppoliki, pointing cautiously to Charles. "His name apparently is Charles Venables, or such like."

Blood stared at Charles for a moment. "Why, that's the Charles Venables who is Lady Viola's friend and a journalist—a gossip-writer," he said at last. "He's no more a detective than I am. I should have thought you would have seen that from one glance at the fellow. Anyone less like a detective—and more like an ass," added the parson, for his nerves had been rattled, "I've never seen."

Eppoliki fluttered his arms with the ready admission of a mistake which is one of the most engaging characteristics of the Oriental.

"Sorry," he said. "You look a little pale, what? Come to my room and have a drink."

VI

The door of the lounge was flung open. An elderly woman was silhouetted in the doorway. Her grey hair was ragged and tousled, and a huge shawl draped her, falling to her feet. Her yellow skin was seamed and lined with innumerable crow's-feet, and her eyes were blank and staring.

"My God, Miss Geranium!" whispered Viola to Charles. "She's seen something again."

"The prophet Ezekiel has just been with me," she announced in tones which were patently modelled on those of a B.B.C. announcer. "He came on a wheel of fire," she added, as if feeling that some further explanation was needed. "He told me that the wrath of the Lord would visit this evil and adulterous generation, and in particular this hotel! 'You are a sinner, Miss Geranium,' he said to me. 'So are we all. But there are sinners in this place who lead others into sin, and on them the vengeance of the Lord will fall.'"

Miss Geranium looked round the ring of embarrassed or mocking eyes. Her assurance seemed to go. "I am sorry if you are not interested," she said pathetically. She paused. "I felt it was a message you all ought to know," she concluded lamely.

Miss Hectoring went to her side. "It's lovely out now, dear," she said. "I think we will go for a walk."

Chapter Two

PUZZLE—FIND THE BODY

In the best bedroom of the Budges' suite, which formed an exiguous top floor—almost an attic—to the Garden Hotel, Mrs Budge was lying with flushed face and open mouth. She stared at the wall with vacant eyes while the daily routine of the sick-room went on oiled gears under the oversight of the efficient Nurse Evans.

There was a knock on the door, and the nurse went out to the sitting-room to speak to Miss Sanctuary. Miss Sanctuary had come to give the nurse half an hour's rest while she sat with Mrs Budge.

She knew something about nursing—during the war she had been a V.A.D.—and the nurse was glad to snatch what she invariably described as forty winks while the old lady sat by her patient over a book.

Nurse Evans went into the sitting-room and looked at her watch. It was close on nine. The watch was a repeater, and she set it for nine-thirty. Then, dropping into a chair, she closed her eyes.

Ten minutes later Miss Sanctuary put her head round the door.

"Where can I get a clean teaspoon?" she asked.

There was no reply, except for a rhythmic hissing from Nurse Evans's open lips.

Miss Sanctuary smiled and shut the door.

The hand on Nurse Evans's gold watch, the gift of a grateful patient, crept slowly round the dial. At half-past nine a small tooth geared to the hands released the trigger of the striking mechanism. There was a tinkling sound. Nurse Evans, trained by habit, heard it through the mists of sleep and was wide awake.

She looked up, and as she did so saw Miss Sanctuary's smiling face round the door.

"The patient's sleeping nicely," she said.

At that moment occurred the event which even then made Nurse Evans think that she was still dreaming, that still comes back to her in sleep and drowsiness with the compelling reality of nightmare.

Even while Miss Sanctuary leant round the door, smiling rosily at her, a gloved hand emerged round the edge of the door and fastened about her throat. The woman's expression changed with the rapidity of a lightning flash. She gave one long-drawn scream closed by a gurgle, and then she was dragged back behind the door, out of sight. The door slammed to, and Nurse Evans, who had risen to her feet, met only the blank wood of the door. With a queer chill feeling and trembling legs, she tried the handle. It was locked.

She beat violently at the door, and she heard a strange voice crying, "Who's there?" Dully she realized it was her own voice...

Nurse Evans was frightened but still cool-headed. Next to the sitting-room, although not forming part of the suite, was a smaller bedroom, in which Budge was sleeping during the illness of his wife. The outer wall of this room, with its big french windows and verandah, was at right angles to the outer wall (also with its window and verandah) of the bedroom in which Mrs Budge was lying. Mrs Budge's bed was near the window, and in changing the invalid's sheets she had noticed that it was possible to see right into the other bedroom. It now occurred to her that the reverse should hold good, and that she should be able to see into Mrs Budge's room. It took her a matter of seconds to decide this and go out into the main corridor into which opened both Mrs Budge's suite and this neighbouring bedroom.

As she opened the sitting-room door she heard a door close and saw moving down the corridor the retreating figure of Mr Budge.

"Quick," she screamed, "something terrible has happened in Mrs Budge's room!"

Without waiting for a reply, she dashed into the smaller bedroom, and looked out.

It was dark outside. But through the window which she had opened a light streamed into the darkness. The window of Mrs Budge's bedroom was open too, she could see, and the curtains bellied out, fluttering in the reflected light. But Mrs Budge's room was in darkness.

"What in heaven's name is the matter?" exclaimed Budge, who had joined her at the window.

The nurse pointed dramatically at the darkened bedroom. "There's someone in there who has just attacked Miss Sanctuary," she said. "I tried to go to her help but the door was locked, and I can't get any answer." Frightened though she was, she couldn't resist the melodramatic touch now that she had an audience. Her pale, discreetly powdered face took on an expression of morbid sympathy. "Something terrible has happened, I'm certain," she stated in a low tone.

Budge's face turned the colour of his deep upstanding collar. "Good God, they've got her," he exclaimed and shambled into the sitting-room.

Though his frame was lanky, with spindly legs and long arms, Budge's chest and shoulders told of not inconsiderable strength. He shook the door with sullen fury, and for a moment it looked as if he would hurl himself bodily at it, or batter it down with a chair.

Then he flung himself at the bureau and pulled a revolver out of the top drawer. Shades of Hollywood—Nurse Evans's eyes protruded slightly and her legs trembled.

Budge flung out of the sitting-room door. Nurse Evans eagerly followed him. He hurriedly locked the neighbouring bedroom door and returned with the key.

"That'll hold them for a little," he muttered. He went to the inner door. "Now then," he admonished through the chink, "I'm going to blast this lock off."

In the little room the sound was deafening. Twice Budge fired and the acrid smoke made Nurse Evans cough.

The lock was half splintered out of the door and the handle was ludicrously twisted. Budge kicked it open, at the same time falling back, revolver in hand.

The light from the sitting-room shone into the bedroom, gleaming on polished mahogany, illuminating the mirror of the huge wardrobe, whitening the pages of the book which lay open on the chair beside the bed. The pages of the book blew over one by one with a faint ruffling noise as the curtains fluttered in a gust of wind.

But the chair was empty, and so was the bed, its clothes turned down. And even in the shadows of the room there was no assailant concealed and no invalid, and no Miss Sanctuary.

Wildly, in that anti-climax, Nurse Evans thought of a nursery rhyme of her youth.

But when she got there the cupboard was bare.

"They've got her all right," mumbled Mr Budge. His sudden energy had spent itself. "Which one of them is it?"

I I

"I wonder how Mrs Budge is?" said Mrs Walton, shuffling the cards meditatively.

"Probably sleeping peaceful," answered her opponent, Eppoliki. "I spoke to Dr Clout—prognosis on the whole favourable." His tone was authoritative, with a tincture of condescension, as became a medical student who had already failed three times to obtain from King's College the right to add the letters M.B. to his name. "There is, of course," he added, "always a distinct possibility of pyæmia, what?"

"Oh, dear," said Mrs Walton; "is that dangerous?"

Charles had intuitions. Perhaps, as he afterwards claimed, he was *en rapport* with his partner; although the state of the score hardly confirmed this. But he had a sudden suspicion that Mrs Walton's idle enough remark was prompted not by sympathy, but by hope. This was by no means to be read crudely in her face. That face, with the swimming eyes and candid curves of a Greuze beauty, was more naturally accessible to sympathy than vindictiveness. But as there suddenly might flash into the liquid eyes of a deer a red spark of defiance, Charles saw in Mrs Walton's eyes a flicker of something akin to hate—fear cornered and with its back to the wall.

Charles's intuitions had cost him so much at bridge that he did not greatly trust them in life. But he filed the idea away in his mind for future reference, and picked up his hand.

"Pyæmia," explained Eppoliki. He licked his lips, and his glass eye, which dirt or age had caused to become slightly filmed, stared into space, while the other swivelled rapidly round the company at the bridge table. By a fortunate chance he had done some clinical work on pyæmia that very day. He embarked joyously into the details. "And so you get all this pus," he wound up.

"Two spades," remarked the dealer, Colonel Cantrip, in a firm voice, and with such a depth of meaning in his intonation that Eppoliki realized at once that the call had some esoteric significance.

"A forcing bid," he sighed to himself and re-examined his hand. Forcing bids worried him. The East does not like to be forced, and Eppoliki had already indicated this by one or two calls of such a nature that at the end of the hand his opponents had watched anxiously the struggle between good manners and apoplexy flaming in the Colonel's face.

Viola lay back in her chair, waiting to cut in. Meanwhile she amused herself by watching the play and attempting to gauge the players' characters from their hands.

The twinkle in Eppoliki's eye showed that he refused to regard any game in which skill, however mingled with chance, played a part, as anything more than a game. Not so his partner. Colonel Cantrip's play was devoid of insight but inevitably correct. He counted his honour tricks with the same rigid exactitude as he had calculated elevation and direction when he was a young gunnery officer. Nothing in heaven or earth would, Viola was sure, have induced him to overstep the permitted bounds.

Charles was capable of anything. At the moment, for instance, he was two down on his contract as the result of an unnecessary finesse; but his finesses were less exasperating than his psychic bids. Where he knew his opponents well he occasionally showed flashes of diabolical intuition, but when he didn't, as in the present case, he went down with monotonous regularity.

"I am sorry," Charles was explaining. "I thought that as Eppoliki raised his partner to three diamonds he must have had the queen, and raised his partner thinking he had the ace and king."

Following her train of thought, Viola toyed with the idea of a detective who reduced his suspects to three and invited them to a game of bridge. The cards would be stacked to test certain qualities whose possession would identify the criminal.

"Of course people like Mrs Walton are hopeless," she decided. "She plays absolutely by rule of thumb, invariably leading through strength and up to weakness regardless of—"

A loud report startled them. It was followed in a moment by another. The noise seemed to come from overhead.

Charles put down his hand disgustedly. "A loud shot rang out! This is too bad," he said. "In another moment or two a masked man will walk in."

Mrs Walton laughed, but not altogether naturally. "Surely that was a burst tyre or an engine back-firing or something."

"You're right m'boy," exclaimed the Colonel, laying down his cards also. He pulled at his moustache. "You can't tell me much about gun-fire. That was a firearm—revolver or small-bore rifle—and it was in this house..."

The door was flung open. Budge walked in.

"My wife!" he exclaimed. The first glance showed Charles that this was a badly scared man. "Something terrible has happened to her." His gaze wandered round the room, falling for a moment on each member of the company in turn.

He addressed Cantrip. "Will you come upstairs with me?" he said.

The Colonel rose to his feet.

The same thought was in everyone's eyes. The pleurisy, in spite of Dr Clout's assurances, had taken a fatal turn. The Colonel, however, it was to be assumed, had looked on death unshaken. "Right, Budge," he said. "Keep calm. I'll come."

Eppoliki followed him. "Pyæmia," he muttered to himself. "Very interesting."

Charles, however, realized that no ordinary visit of death could have induced Budge to rush in this way into a room full of his guests and call for aid. The correct thing to do was to ring up the doctor and eventually the undertaker and let the whole thing run on the oiled wheels of custom. Budge could be relied upon to do the correct thing.

Mrs Walton said nothing. As he closed the door he saw her, eyes fixed on vacancy, steadily shuffling the cards, over and over again.

III

"There's something terrible happened, Colonel, of that I'm sure," said Budge for the second time, as he concluded the story, corroborated and supplemented by Evans, of the disappearance of Mrs Budge and Miss Sanctuary from behind locked doors.

The ruffled bed-clothes and the spread-eagled novel were the only signs of a struggle. Not that the furniture was of the light kind that would have suffered from any but the fiercest of affrays. The huge mahogany wardrobe which dominated the room would have completely filled the drawing-room of an ordinary flat. The now empty bed was of the deep Victorian variety whose depths of mattress promised a comfort not always fulfilled. Two high chairs, with much-carven backs, faced the fire, whose leaping flames were reflected in the varnished gloom of the Lincrusta'd walls.

A vast mahogany roll-top desk stood in the corner, and the wall opposite the window was obstructed, for the greater part of its length, by a fine specimen of the now extinct horsehair sofa. The contrast to the chromium-plated and unpolished-wood style of decoration of the rest of the house was patent, and suggested a sort of "lost plateau" of Victorianism, surviving in the proprietorial fastnesses of the Garden Hotel.

"Well, people can't vanish like smoke," snorted Cantrip. "Now if the door was really locked they must have got through the window. If she was well enough to walk she got out herself, probably followed by Miss Sanctuary. If not, she must have got out with Miss Sanctuary."

"Or," said Eppoliki pleasantly, "they were both knocked on the head and their bodies flung out of the window."

With a common movement the five went out on to the verandah.

The storey which formed the private suite of the Budges in the Garden Hotel was really a sort of minor gabled projection in the roof. Although the two verandahs were almost contiguous, and one could easily leap from one to the other, there were no other projections for two storeys down, where, from the first floor, emerged an outer iron staircase leading into the paved yard.

It was plain that whoever tried to escape from the verandah of either room into the yard would, unless he were an acrobat, have the greatest difficulty in getting down safely. It was even more difficult to imagine a middle-aged invalid and an elderly spinster clambering down into the garden, even with the strongest of motives.

"What's that?" exclaimed Nurse Evans excitedly.

They stared down into the gloom beneath. Here and there a light shone in the rooms of the hotel. The rays from the window, aided by the moonlight, feebly illuminated the paved yard below.

"Look there!" she said, pointing. "Huddled over in the corner."

Charles inspected it with his monocle. "It does look rather like an old lady," he admitted, "but I'm afraid it's only a motor-cycle covered by a tarpaulin. Those sinister-looking figures on the opposite side are also bogus, I am afraid. Closer inspection would only prove them to be dust-bins."

"Well, it's very extraordinary," remarked the Colonel, harping on the point. "The door was locked. They've gone. Where? Through the window, of course, but where?" It was obvious, although he was too much of a gentleman to put it into words, that it was very reprehensible of two ladies of mature years to vanish into thin air while he was playing bridge. "And again *why*?" he went on. "But of course they were attacked," he admitted generously, "forced to do it—that's about the size of it."

No one disagreed with the Colonel. "Whatever the purpose of their little jaunt," remarked Charles, "their most obvious route is to pop into this next verandah—a little jump would clear the gap—through the open window and so back into the corridor. Though why that should really help them, I don't know."

Nurse Evans remembered the closing door and the retreating figure of Mr Budge.

"Mr Budge is using that room now," she remarked. "He was in there at the time Miss Sanctuary was attacked, I think."

The eyes of the company focussed on Mr Budge. He did not look happy under the scrutiny.

"No," he protested. "Oh, no."

Nurse Evans persisted. Professional discretion was all very well, but drama was in the air.

"When I was coming out of the room I heard the door close," she stated, "and when I looked out you were going downstairs."

Budge looked annoyed. He glared sullenly at the nurse.

"I was coming up," he asserted.

"Well, all I can say is it must have been very awkward," she muttered.

"Awkward," trumpeted the Colonel, "what do you mean—awkward?"

"Coming upstairs backwards," she said triumphantly. "Anyway, it looks as if my job here is ended," she thought to herself. "Coming upstairs indeed!"

Budge appeared discomfited. He hesitated for a moment, and then laughed nervously. "I think you are mistaken. However, I went into my bedroom a little earlier to fetch a newspaper I left there. I did not stay long and I noticed nothing out of the way while I was in there. I was coming back about ten minutes later when Nurse Evans rushed out."

"How long were you in the room altogether?" asked Charles.

"About two minutes," he answered. There was a wary gleam in his eye.

Charles turned to the nurse. "How long was it after hearing Miss Sanctuary scream that you saw Mr Budge?"

The nurse thought. "About five minutes. I was a long time trying to get the door opened."

The fact that Budge was under suspicion slowly seemed to sink into the Colonel's understanding. He looked sternly at Budge.

"Come now, Budge," he pressed. "Didn't you hear anything when you were coming upstairs?"

"No, I didn't," snapped the other, "and I resent your manner, Colonel. Are you suggesting that I have made away with my wife and Miss Sanctuary? If so, can you tell me how I made them vanish into thin air?"

"That's true, Budge, very true." The Colonel wagged his head. "Where could they—"

His sentence was interrupted by a cry from the nurse, who had returned into the bedroom.

"There's something moving in here!"

Charles leaped into the room.

A sigh and a muffled groan, like the despairing cry of a vanished ghost, hung in the air.

Charles leaped to the huge wardrobe. The door was locked, but the key was in it. He turned it and swung open the door.

He was looking straight into a face—the flushed, gagged face of Miss Sanctuary. As he opened the door, against which her knees had been braced, she shot out of the wardrobe and dropped into Charles's arms, panting but inert. She was bound hand and foot.

Chapter Three

ENTER THE POLICE

Willing hands helped the old lady on to the bed; and while Charles loosened the scientifically tied rope, the nurse chafed her feet and hands, which were numb from the arrested circulation.

"God bless my soul," remarked the Colonel, "they tied her up and put her in the cupboard!"

For a moment it looked as if Miss Sanctuary was going to faint. Eppoliki dashed some water in her face and she sat up. Her eyes were dazed and for a moment she did not seem to recognize where she was.

"Now, Miss Sanctuary," said the Colonel, "if you are better will you please tell us what happened?"

She passed her hand over her eyes and smiled weakly. "I am afraid I am not going to be very helpful," she said. "While I was sitting with Mrs Budge I thought I heard a noise in the room, but decided it was only the furniture creaking. Then when I went to speak to Nurse Evans I was seized from behind and, at the same time, the lights were put out."

She smiled reminiscently. "I struggled quite hard, but I am afraid I did not last long. I fell down and struck my head, and while I was being tied up I must have fainted. The next thing I knew was that I was in the cupboard, terribly cramped, and wondering where on earth I was."

She looked round the room. "Did they attack Mrs Budge too?" she asked. "Where is she?"

"We don't know what has happened to Mrs Budge," answered the Colonel portentously. "She has disappeared."

"Disappeared? Good heavens, where?"

Miss Sanctuary was badly shaken by the news. She lay back, pallid, her eyes closed.

"We must act," said the Colonel decisively. "Budge, you must go all over the hotel and find out whether there is any trace of your wife or whether anybody has seen or heard anything." He paused impressively. "A dangerous man is at large. The guests will have to be warned, and gathered together in the lounge until the police arrive."

He turned to Eppoliki. "Eppoliki, see that no one is allowed in or out of the building. Get the staff to guard the doors."

"Venables! Where's Venables got to? Oh, there you are!" Charles had just returned after slipping downstairs to phone his news editor to hold the front page for a big story. "Venables, phone the police and tell them to come round at once. I shall stay here with Miss Sanctuary," he declared. "Send the police up the moment they arrive."

II

Charles had collected Viola on his way back. Mrs Walton had disappeared.

"What a fantastic story," Viola exclaimed. "It seems almost too incredible. There we were playing bridge while Mrs Budge is whisked away."

She reflected for a moment. "I suppose the obvious deduction is that something pretty terrible has happened to Mrs Budge."

Charles dropped for a moment his air of levity. "I don't like it. It is just conceivable that Mrs Budge is all right. On the other hand, the *mise en scène* has the romantic air of a 'crook' thriller, and one's police-court experience has taught one that the really dangerous crook is inclined to model himself on fiction."

He paused a moment. "The most obvious explanation of the whole thing is that Mrs Budge attacked Miss Sanctuary, tied her up, and then escaped." He paused regretfully. "It is a pity there are certain flaws in the theory. The alternative theory is, of course, that somebody was hiding in the cupboard, and carried away Mrs Budge dead or persuaded her to come away with them alive."

He sighed. "I have a strong feeling that the police are not going to have an easy task. It is a safe bet that Budge and his party won't find anything. The man must have foreseen the need for escape."

"What a cold-blooded way you talk about it," commented Viola. "I suppose that's the result of being a journalist."

"Of course, the alternative is that the man's a maniac. If Mrs Budge has intruded into the world of fantasy of some homicidal lunatic, the trail is going to be more difficult still."

III

Breathing heavily, the Colonel was seated at the sitting-room table, making notes for the benefit of the police. The death-or-glory soldiers of Waterloo were followed by another and alien generation who fought principally on paper. Each bullet that went pinging on the enemy parapet, each sandbag which shielded the heads of the infantrymen, and the life and death of every living unit in the army, was guided to its appointed destiny by the pen wielded by some red-tabbed staff officer or the typewriter strummed by some perspiring N.C.O. True to this great military tradition, the Colonel was getting things down on paper.

Charles leaned over his shoulder. "The real military touch," he said. "One spinster cased and corded, for the use of, damaged. Now wait until you see my version in to-morrow's *Mercury*. The most astounding disappearance ever recorded in the annals of London crime took place yesterday in the suite of a Kensington hotel, when Mrs Budge, the proprietress…"

The Colonel had treated Charles with the good-humoured kindness one accords to the mentally deficient or the very young ever since he had remarked brightly, "Kiss the dealer," when the two, three, and four of hearts had fallen to the Colonel's ace in the course of their game of bridge.

"Did you telephone the police?" he asked coldly.

"O.K., Chief," replied Charles, springing smartly to attention. "They are sending round two of the best brains of Lancaster Gate."

"We will need them," replied the Colonel seriously. "D'ye know, Venables, I should be extremely surprised if Budge and his party found anything. But it will narrow down times and so forth for the police when they arrive."

Charles looked at him with a new respect.

IV

The atmosphere of the Garden Hotel had become extremely tense. As Budge and his assistants went round from room to room and warned everyone they met, the lounge grew crowded with people almost inarticulate with excitement. Practically everyone had remembered a different version of the story told them, and as these accounts were collated, embellished and repeated, the story of the day's happenings grew more unrecognizable and terrifying with every passing minute.

Mr Nicholas Twing, the manager of a big financial house in the City, stood with his back to the wall and a breast-pocket stuffed with papers, swinging a poker menacingly in one hand. The Rev. Septimus Blood also carried valuables in the shape of a pyx, two chalices, a richly ornamented burse, and a golden offertory plate which he had wrapped in his underclothes and packed in a large sponge bag.

If the six masked intruders (for this was the number on which the majority of stories agreed) had penetrated to the lounge, they would probably have found little difficulty in overcoming the resistance of both these gentlemen. They might have hesitated, however, at the sight of Miss Hectoring who, with Miss Geranium clinging to her left arm, brandished in her sword-arm a foil from which the button had been torn. Her moustache bristled with pugnacity and her frontal development bore witness to her expertness and assiduity in the use of the weapon she was wielding.

On the sofa sat Mrs Walton and Mrs Salterton-Deeley under the protection of Mr Winterton, a bald and whiskered old gentleman who, as the father-in-law of Sir Henry Claygate, the poet laureate, might have been one of the lions of the hotel were it not for his deafening table manners. Now, however, he was affording protection to the two ladies by his side while Mrs Salterton-Deeley, as a second line of defence, was busily making up her face.

In spite of the instructions to residents to assemble in the lounge, the panic had spread in a small measure to the Budges' suite where Cantrip, Venables and Viola waited for the police, while Eppoliki and Nurse Evans looked after the prostrate Miss Sanctuary.

The panic took the form of Miss Mumby, who burst into the room followed by five cats, and with three kittens in her arms. These she deposited on the table where, after a preliminary canter, they seized the Colonel's pen and dribbled it smartly round the table. It left an inky smear across the Colonel's carefully drafted report.

"My children must be protected from this monster, Colonel," she announced. "So I have brought them here."

"Your children," echoed the Colonel, somewhat taken aback.

"Yes, my little family," replied Miss Mumby. "Now then, Snowball and Susie, leave the Colonel's pen alone! Walter, I'm surprised at you! Where are your table manners?"

"The villains who have spirited away Mrs Budge," she went on, having reduced the three kittens to mewling quiescence, "might not hesitate to hurt my cats."

"At the present moment, madam," replied Cantrip with justifiable annoyance, "we would be only too glad to come across the man or men responsible for the assault on Miss Sanctuary and the disappearance of Mrs Budge. So far no trace of them or of Mrs Budge has been discovered in the hotel. The scent is cold now, I'm afraid."

"How can you expect to find them?" said Miss Mumby warmly, forgetting her fright for the moment. "Have you the instincts with which an animal is gifted by nature?"

"No," snapped the Colonel. "I'm not a bloodhound, if that's what you mean."

"Of course not. Now if Mrs Budge is in this building, Socrates will be able to trace her. Come here, Socrates."

During the conversation Miss Mumby's five cats had leaped on to the sofa between Viola and Charles, and lay there without any further sign of movement than an occasional twitch of the ear or icy glare of disapproval at the misbehaving Walter, who had resumed possession of the Colonel's pen and was meditatively chewing the end. Socrates, a large black tom-cat with a torn ear, sprang from the sofa and went to his mistress's side.

"Socrates has been trained to be a tracker," explained Miss Mumby proudly. "If you give him some belonging of Mrs Budge's to sniff, Socrates will track her down."

Charles was immensely tickled by the idea and persuaded Eppoliki, who had left Miss Sanctuary to the care of Nurse Evans, to fetch some article of clothing belonging to the vanished proprietress. Miss Mumby watched with approval. She had a tremendous respect for Egyptians, whom she vaguely believed still worshipped cats. She also knew a medium whose "control" was a Pharaoh, who showed himself possessed of a penetrating insight into her affairs.

Eppoliki returned with a pair of gloves. Miss Mumby explained the situation briefly to Socrates, who watched her with unwinking eyes, and appeared to understand every word, and then she gave him the gloves to sniff. Socrates danced round the room on the tips of his toes, twitching his tail and snuffling loudly, and then dashed into the bedroom. Miss Sanctuary, apparently slightly better, was still lying on Mrs Budge's bed with her head up. Socrates dashed wildly round the room twice, and then leapt with a throaty cry of triumph on to Miss Sanctuary's chest.

"Damn the animal," exclaimed this overwrought lady, and Socrates immediately leapt off again and retired under the wardrobe.

Miss Sanctuary apparently belonged to the type of old maid who intensely dislikes cats, and she insisted on Socrates being taken away, even after his bloodhound propensities had been explained to her. Cantrip retired in disgust, but Charles refused to be discouraged and, accompanied by Miss Mumby and Viola, carried Socrates out on to the verandah, shutting the french windows behind them.

"Mrs Budge must have gone through the window," he explained, "and we should be able to pick up the trail here."

Socrates, with waving tail, encouraged by his mistress, walked all round the balustrade and leapt lightly into the balcony leading into the other bed-room. From here he leapt on to a cornice on the story below, and from there dropped ten feet on to a drain-pipe cover. He did not stop there, but scrambled down the drain-pipe and jumped on to the edge of the outer iron staircase which ran from the first floor to the yard. The three on the balcony leaned over the edge, until he went outside the rays from the two windows and was lost to sight.

"If that was the route followed by Mrs Budge," remarked Charles, "she must be an angel or an acrobat."

"Socrates is certainly on the scent of something," declared Miss Mumby positively. "His tail was twitching, and it never does unless he is on a trail."

In a few moments Socrates' black body slunk into the rays from the window, which lit the head of the fire-escape. Once again he got on the drain-pipe cover, swarmed up the pipe itself to the cornice, and from here manœuvred his way to the verandah.

"By Jove," said Charles, peering intently through his monocle, "the little blighter's carrying something!"

And so he was. Socrates bounded to his mistress's feet and, with every appearance of acute self-satisfaction, deposited there the relics of a haddock, which, to judge from its appearance, he had retrieved from a dust-bin encountered on his journey.

V

"And that is all we know at the moment," concluded Colonel Cantrip, as he finished giving his résumé of the happenings of the evening to Sergeant Noakes.

Police Sergeant Noakes was a conscientious, deliberate policeman, well versed in the technique of his job. He was not intelligent, if intelligence demands a nimble acuteness of perception, but he could be trusted to pursue the tenor of his way without being sidetracked. Charles felt that this ruddy-faced, calm individual was sufficiently representative of the stubborn will and patient driving power of the British police. He made no comment until Colonel Cantrip had finished.

"I should like to hear what the nurse and Mr Budge have to say," said the Sergeant, after writing for a moment in his notebook.

The Sergeant was sitting in the chair vacated by Cantrip, and he motioned the nurse and Mr Budge into the chairs opposite him on the other side of the table.

"Will you tell me exactly what happened, Nurse," he said, "in your own words and time? Tell them exactly as they happened to you without including anything you learned of afterwards."

In a toneless voice the nurse described Miss Sanctuary's offer, and how she left the kind old lady by the patient's bedside. Yes, she had noticed the condition of the patient when she left. Mrs Budge had fallen into a deep sleep. The nurse explained how she had slept for half an hour by her repeater. She had accustomed herself, she explained, to dropping off instantly anywhere. She had been awakened at half-past nine, and had then seen the horrifying assault on Miss Sanctuary.

"I thought that I might be able to see into the room from the bedroom next door and rushed into it. Mr Budge had just left it." (She paused as if expecting a contradiction, but none came.) "The window was wide open, but I could see nothing, except that the light had been turned out."

"Thank you for a very clear statement, Nurse," said the Sergeant. "Did anything occur afterwards of which the Colonel would not know—I mean which might in any way throw light on the disappearance of Mrs Budge?"

After consideration the nurse thought, "No."

"Now, Mr Budge," said the Sergeant, snapping the band of his notebook, "would you kindly tell us your story in the same way?"

"Nurse Evans shouted to me as I was on the stairs," answered Mr Budge, "and I came along—"

"One moment," interrupted the Sergeant. "Would you begin from the beginning? I understand that you were in this room next door."

"Oh," replied Mr Budge, staring at his boots. He hesitated a moment, and then climbed down completely without any explanation. "I did not think that had anything to do with the case. However, about half-past nine—I am not sure of the time—I went to the room next door, which I am using as a bedroom at present, to fetch a newspaper I had left there. I was only in there for a couple of minutes."

The nurse snorted, but made no comment.

"Did you see or hear anything strange from Mrs Budge's room during that time?" he was asked.

"No."

"Did you notice whether the light was on or off?"

"No, I did not."

"Was the window up?"

"I cannot remember."

"Thank you. You were saying Nurse Evans called to you...?"

"I followed her back to my bedroom. She was staring through the window. We went back to the sitting-room and found that my wife's door was locked, as she said, and the key apparently in it on the other side. We could still get no answer to our shouts, and I remembered an automatic that was in our bureau."

The Sergeant raised his eyebrows and said nothing.

"I haven't a licence for it, I'm afraid," Budge added, interpreting the look. "I thought it better not to risk trying to climb in through the window, so I locked the door of the other bedroom to cut off one channel of escape, and then blew the lock off the door in here. The rest Nurse Evans has already told you. Then I fetched the Colonel, and he has told you how we found Miss Sanctuary. I went round the hotel searching for any trace of my wife. We found none. At the same time I warned the guests and told them to assemble in the lounge until the police came."

"I noticed them as I came in," said the Sergeant dryly. "They appeared to be alarmed."

"As I say, I found no trace of my wife," went on Mr Budge, "and no one, so far as I could gather, had seen or heard anything strange."

Mr Budge gave his evidence very much as if he were describing the plot of a play he had seen. As he sat there, with his dry, rasping voice, his Adam's apple bobbing industriously behind his white collar, he reminded the observer more than ever of some pillar of a Nonconformist chapel. The Sergeant was familiar with his type, but had to admit that the coolness of his action in the emergency was unexpected. That revolver, too...

Charles, remembering the conversation overheard the previous day, believed that his story had been carefully rehearsed and might conceal anything or nothing, but that, at any rate, Budge was consciously feeling his way across slippery places.

The Sergeant made no comment, but turned to the constable with him. "Phone the Station," he said, "and ask them to send up six more men."

During the conversation Charles had been making notes of the leading points of the statement in a slim notebook. He had caught the Sergeant's eye upon him once or twice, but had consciously evaded it. The Police Sergeant now stared hard at him.

"Excuse me, sir," he said, "but what might those notes be for?"

"For my story for the *Mercury*," replied Charles calmly.

Noakes looked disconcerted.

"I propose to phone through my story," went on Charles, "but I should like you to hear the main points before I do so."

"Now then, Mr—"

"Venables."

"Mr Venables, you know perfectly well I can't give you any official release at this stage of the investigation. I can't stop you putting anything you like in your paper, but you're responsible for it."

"I realize that, Officer," Charles answered. "I merely want to know whether anything I am going to say is likely to hinder you in any way."

"All right," said the Sergeant, somewhat mollified, "fire away…"

A few minutes later Charles rose to go. Just before he went out he turned to the Sergeant. "In your own interests, Sergeant," he said dramatically, "there is one thing I must draw your attention to. Have you examined the top right-hand panel on that door?"

Following his pointing finger, the occupants of the room gazed in unison at the panel to see what had attracted Charles's attention. He took advantage of the lull to sweep off the side table a silver-framed photograph of Mrs Budge, and passed quietly out of the room to the nearest telephone.

VI

The men the Sergeant had sent for soon arrived. Two he placed on guard at the back and front doors to replace the voluntary guards posted by the Colonel. Viola, Eppoliki, the Colonel and Budge he sent downstairs to join the crowd in the lounge, whose fear by this time had been completely overcome by their curiosity. The newcomers were fully occupied in endeavouring to communicate a truthful account of the events of the evening.

The Sergeant went in to Miss Sanctuary with the nurse. Miss Sanctuary was feeling very ill indeed now, and the shock of her experience, as so often happens, was beginning to manifest itself some time after the event.

With an obvious effort she pulled herself together for a moment, and told the Sergeant the story which she had told before but which the Sergeant had only heard from hearsay.

When he had heard out her story the Sergeant proceeded to interrogate her.

"Have you any ideas as to the identity of your assailant?"

"None."

"Man or woman?"

"I feel certain it was a man," said Miss Sanctuary. "I have no definite reason, but the grip of the hands, the material of the cuffs that brushed my cheek when I was bound, and the tread, make me positive it was a man."

The Sergeant put many leading questions, but he was able to extract nothing which gave any definite pointer to the size or even the build of the intruder. Any conclusions he would form were based on deduction, and the Sergeant loathed deduction.

"Would you swear in a court of law that it was a man?"

Miss Sanctuary remained silent for a moment. The Sergeant could watch, in the alterations of her expression, her reconstruction of the sudden attack.

"No," she said at last. "I would not swear more than that I had the impression that it was a man."

"When you were locked in the cupboard what could you hear?"

"I have a faint recollection of hearing a tramp of feet, and a dragging noise," she said. "I believe I could also hear Nurse Evans shouting and banging on the door. Then it was that I fainted again, I think."

"Thank you, Miss Sanctuary," said the Sergeant, "that will be all for the moment. Would you like to go back to your room?"

"I'll stay here till I feel a bit stronger," she said. "I am afraid my old bones are rather shaken."

Going into the sitting-room, the Sergeant put his best man in charge of a search-party to turn out every inch of the hotel, accompanied by Mr Budge.

The Sergeant returned and made a methodical search of the room. Four possible hiding-places struck his eye. He looked under the bed, under the sofa, in the wardrobe, and in a large laundry basket which stood beside it.

Mr Budge was not content to be the hotel proprietress's husband. He ran a laundry, which every guest of the Garden Hotel was expected to use. A laundry basket of gargantuan dimensions and ornamental design stood in each bedroom, and the Sergeant reflected that it would be an ideal place to hide in for a small man, but difficult to get out of quickly and quietly. The verandah came in for close inspection, and in the same way he examined the sitting-room and then went into the next-door bedroom. He flashed a torch round the balustrade and examined the likely hiding-places. It was plain from his puzzled expression when he returned to Miss Sanctuary that he had seen nothing which formed a plausible basis for a working theory.

"The cupboard is the most obvious place to hide in," he concluded. "Ten to one that's where he was."

"Have you found anything, Sergeant?" she asked with a pale smile.

"I have found lots of things," he replied cheerily. "But I am not yet prepared to say whether they have any bearing on the case! I am going downstairs now to see the rest of the residents, and afterwards I may want another word with you."

Miss Sanctuary's smile went, and she rose painfully from the bed. "Don't leave me alone," she said. "I feel that awful man is still around." She shuddered.

"You needn't worry," he replied. "It is obvious that Mrs Budge, and not you, was the object of the attack. In any case, it is unlikely that he is still in the building. However, there will be a man on duty in the corridor at the door, and at a word from you he will come in. As soon as you feel better I should go back to your room."

Miss Sanctuary seemed relieved. "Thank you," she smiled. "I think I shall feel safer if I lock the doors all the same." She lay back.

The Sergeant walked out of the room, and after a few words of instruction to the man on duty outside the suite, went downstairs to the rest of the residents.

VII

"Up to a late hour," Charles phoned, "not a sign, not the faintest clue to the whereabouts of Mrs Budge has been discovered. The mystery bids fair to be one of the most baffling of modern times. Our special correspondent, who was first on the spot, and who interviewed Miss Sanctuary, is in close touch with the police, and is playing a part in the investigations."

"Right," said Meredith, at the other end of the wire, as he tore the last page of copy out of the silent typing machine and handed it to the sub behind him.

Three minutes later it was in front of the linotype operator.

"Hold on a moment," said Meredith, "Mr Bailey wants to speak to you."

Charles heard the news editor's congratulations with real elation.

"A first-rate story," grunted Bailey. "You're wasted on society stuff. Get your nose on the scent of this story and keep it there. Oh, by the way, the art editor's at my elbow and says can you get a photo of Mrs Budge?"

"I've got one in my pocket now," replied Charles proudly. "I pinched it in full view of the police. Send round a messenger in a taxi and it will be waiting."

"Stout fellow," commented Bailey.

Even as they spoke the papier mâché flong was being pressed on to the gleaming type to make the matrix. Soon the stereos would be fixed to the great rollers and the huge cylinders of "British Paper for the *Mercury*" would be converted into penny messengers which would bring to over 1,635,432 homes (excluding all free and unsold copies) the first breath-taking news of the Garden Hotel Mystery; news soon to be followed by developments which would make Charles's first crimson story pale to a watery pink.

Less hurried, but more conscientiously, the process of the law was taking its course. Patiently the Sergeant was examining the crowd in the lounge, endeavouring to extract from them some useful and valid framework of times and places on which to found subsequent investigations. Slowly the search-party combed out the Garden Hotel...

It was well on into the small hours of the morning that the Sergeant returned to his rooms in Glossop Road. His wife had left a thermos flask of hot coffee and a plate of sandwiches, and with these by his side he composed the report which, allied with subsequent developments, was sufficient to bring Detective Inspector Bernard Bray of Scotland Yard to investigate the mystery personally.

Chapter Four

SCOTLAND YARD IS INTERESTED

Extracts from Sergeant Noakes's Report

" At 21.45 of October 29th, I was rung up by a man, who said he was speaking from the Garden Hotel, to report the disappearance of proprietress. Accompanied by Police Constable Chingley I went round, and at 22.00 arrived at the scene of the alleged disappearance…"

(Here followed a summary of the events already recorded.)

"…Although I have interviewed the residents and obtained a rough idea of their movements at the time, the problem mainly centres round the Budges' suite. This, it should be explained, occupies the top floor, which rises out of the main mass of the building and has only three rooms.

"Somebody gained entrance to Mrs Budge's bedroom or was already in the room at 21.30. If he or they were not already in the room (and the possible hiding-places are such that this supposition is doubtful), entrance must have been effected either past the sleeping nurse, or else through the adjoining bedroom via the verandahs.

"The intruder (assuming it a one-man show for the sake of simplicity) must have either carried Mrs Budge off and escaped through the verandahs and adjoining bedroom again, or through the sitting-room while the nurse was out of it.

"Either hypothesis argues an extraordinarily strong and swift worker, aided by luck.

"In a case of this sort, of course, it is possible that the disappearance is a voluntary one. It is conceivable, for instance, that it was Mrs Budge herself who attacked Miss Sanctuary, and then escaped. Mrs Budge was ill with pleurisy at the time, and in addition Miss Sanctuary is of the opinion that her assailant was a man.

"It may be that Mrs Budge voluntarily accompanied the man who attacked Miss Sanctuary.

"While any hypothesis of Mrs Budge accompanying him voluntarily makes simpler the rapidity of the escape, it makes it more remarkable that they were able to get clean out of the building without detection. Also from my conversation with the doctor, I cannot believe it likely that Mrs Budge was sufficiently well to leave her bed voluntarily, and go skylarking over verandahs.

"All stations have been circulated with a description of Mrs Budge, and the usual routine inquiries have been made.

"An examination of the rooms and the hotel produced no clues of significance so far. If Mrs Budge has been forcibly abducted therefore, the only help likely to be forthcoming inside the hotel is from information about Mrs Budge, which may bring out some plausible motive. As in most of these cases of disappearance, however, the source from which information is most likely to come is the Force's routine investigation.

"Two men are at present on duty in the hotel, at the request of Mr Budge.

"(Signed) STANLEY NOAKES, *Sergeant*,
"*Metropolitan Police, Division X.*"

II

The report in the circumstances was a creditable concoction. So thought Detective Inspector Bernard Bray, C.I.D., as he read it next day sitting in his tiny office at Scotland Yard. Nothing in the policeman's purview is more monotonous, however, than a disappearance, which always starts so dramatically and ends so tamely. People rarely disappeared for any but strictly personal reasons. There were remarkable features in the case certainly, and the press were playing them for all they were worth. That was why the report had come direct to Bray, and why his lean face, with its good profile—the face of a barrister rather than of a policeman—was furrowed with a frown of concentration. At four o'clock he would have to see Superintendent Etherton and give an opinion on the case. Meanwhile he literally pigeon-holed it in his capacious desk in favour of an expert's autopsy report.

"It is almost incredible," he said to his assistant, "that poisoners should go on using arsenic and criminals should go on leaving finger-prints in this year of grace. Well, it makes our task easier, I suppose."

"I've sometimes wondered, sir," replied his young assistant, "whether there are so many arsenic poisoning cases, because those are the only cases that are discovered. In the same way, perhaps, the criminal is traced so often by finger-prints, because it is only criminals that leave finger-prints who are caught."

Bray glanced at him keenly. "It's an ingenious theory, Cuff, and one which has sometimes worried me in my more despondent moments. I've come to the conclusion, however, that if we really believed it we might as well throw up our jobs here."

He immersed himself again in the poisoning case. Outside traffic moved up and down London river, sirens moaned, cars hooted. Inside a drama of covetousness, hate, and death had been reduced to the verdict of a physician on the entrails of the deceased. Macbeth, thought Bray, reduced to the terms of a butcher's shop.

It was 3.45 and he had got as far as the liver of the deceased ("definitely positive results were obtained from the Hans-Browning reaction…") when the phone bell rang.

Sergeant Noakes was at the end of the wire. Had anyone been overlooking Bray they would have seen his lips purse in a whistle of excitement and his eyes glitter. "This sounds like a real case," he said, making rapid notes on a pad. He rang off and, seizing the Sergeant's report from its pigeon-hole, committed it to memory, while Superintendent Etherton in his larger, but still sufficiently small room, gazed impatiently at his memorandum pad, which bore accusingly a notation of an appointment at four o'clock with Detective Inspector Bray. In a few minutes, however, any annoyance was wiped out by the news brought him by Bray, who in a short time had reduced the facts of the case to passable coherence.

III

Charles clung limply but happily to a telephone and poured out a story whose ripe details enabled the *Mercury*'s best sub to put up headlines of surpassing juiciness.

"You're in great form to-night, Mr Barnard," said the hoary-headed Father of the Chapel as he drove the wedges into the forme, and Barnard, standing on the stone beside him, modestly agreed.

In the ghostly silence of the early morning streets, when Aurora trysts with Tithonus and the shrill voices of humanity seem to invade the silent empire of night with uneasy trepidation, slatternly looking women with tousled hair and shirt-sleeved men with unshaven faces were fixing the *Mercury*'s bills outside the windows of faded tobacconist shops. The early workers stopped, stared, and purchased.

The Garden Hotel Mystery had become a matter of national importance.

Chapter Five

THE MORNING AFTER

Everybody got up surprisingly early for breakfast on the morning following Mrs Budge's disappearance. Charles, who rarely looked at his tongue in the glass before eleven in the morning, found himself beaming over a steaming jug of coffee at Viola at nine o'clock.

"I met one of our heavy-footed friends on the way to my bath," said Charles conversationally. "He was lurking in the linen-room next door with the chambermaid, whom he was doubtless cross-examining. Anyway, there was a great deal of tittering going on. Apparently there is still no sign of Mrs Budge."

"I suppose when they do find her she will only be a body," speculated Viola.

Charles pushed his kidneys away in disgust. "Please," he protested.

At that moment he caught sight of the front page of the *Mercury*, and had he not forgotten the trick, would certainly have blushed. At the same time he had to admit to an acute and simple feeling of pleasure at the sight of his story blazoned across the front page, illustrated by a front view of the Garden Hotel, a close-up of Mr Budge walking down the steps with his hat in front of his face, and the portrait Charles had purloined the night before.

The sedate thoroughfare of Tunbridge Gardens was already blocked by the crowd of sightseers gaping against the area railings of the Garden Hotel.

"I am glad to find that the coffee is good," said Charles, pouring himself out another cup. "It is an excellent tribute to the way this place is run that the disappearance of the proprietress has not disturbed the service of breakfast."

"I wonder you can eat breakfast at all," replied Viola. "I feel we ought to be prowling round doing something. I've a good mind not to go to the studio to-day."

"Well, I'm not going to the office," said Charles. "I'm a crime reporter for the moment, my girl. Little Pouncefoot will have to run my page. It means he will devote six paragraphs to his sweetie, Doris Desirée, but as I've kept the wretched girl out of the gossip for six months I can't really grumble.

"An idea strikes me. Why not run crime gossip on social lines, if, as apparently is the case, society and crime are the only two things the *Mercury*'s reader is interested in? Dropping into the Sailors' Friend at Limehouse, who should I see but Sally, the charming young wife of Bouncing Bill, who is wintering in Dartmoor. Sally is, of course, the daughter of Mr Jim Grimes, whose recent bigamy will be fresh in the memory of the public. Sally was her usual *soignée* self, and shook her finger playfully at me as she abstracted a purse from the pocket of a stranger beside her. It is, by the way, considered perfectly permissible in the most advanced criminal circles to pick a pocket of a person one has not been introduced to. These modern informal ways are very charming."

"Damn," remarked Viola suddenly. She had been paying no attention to Charles's burbling.

"I beg your pardon?" said Charles.

"I faithfully promised to return Mr Blood's stole before breakfast," she explained.

"What did Mr Blood steal before breakfast?" asked Charles, spreading too much butter on his toast.

"No, silly, *stole*—a thing you wear round your neck," replied Viola. "Mr Blood has a rare Byzantine one which is terribly valuable and he gave it to me the other day to use in a drawing I am making for a poster to advertise the Anglo-Byzantine Church Congress at Much Muddleton. Whether I shall ever be paid for it remains to be seen," she added reflectively. "I wish you'd be an angel and get the stole from my room—it's hanging on a chair—and give it back to Blood. You'll find him in his room—he always has breakfast brought up to his room."

As Charles strolled across the lounge, with the stole over his arm, a reporter who had penetrated past the police on duty approached him.

"Excuse me, sir," he said, "but can you give me a few words about the happenings in the hotel yesterday?"

Charles duly admired the dexterity with which he was impalpably drawn aside.

"What paper do you represent?" asked Charles severely, fixing him with his monocle. "I—ah—I should not mind making a brief statement to the *Times*."

"I represent the *Gazette*," answered the reporter, naming the *Mercury*'s 2,104,326 net sale rival.

"In the circumstances I can give you a full personal statement of all that took place here."

The reporter's eyes glittered. He whipped out the professionally inconspicuous little scrap of paper on which he took his notes.

"Yes," said Charles, drawing out from his pocket that morning's *Mercury*, "here it is."

The reporter, an eager young new-comer to the *Gazette*'s staff from the provinces, saw the joke and laughed so much that Charles, quite touched, gave him an account of what had occurred that morning.

11

Blood, like Charles, was a late riser, except on Sundays, and he was seated in a dressing-gown with a breakfast tray beside him, diverting himself with a monograph on "the Streptococcal Ingestion of Enzymes." He looked up in surprise when Charles entered. "Ah, yes, the stole," he said, "a very fine one. That was presented to me for my work in organizing the first Anglo-Byzantine Congress. As a journalist, you will remember it; it caused a great sensation." Charles remembered it. An enthusiastic Evangelical whose mind had become disordered had climbed up one of the pillars that supported the hall in which the meeting was held. Shrieking, "Milliners! Milliners!" he had flung into the audience articles of feminine clothing of dubious respectability at such a time and place.

While Charles was conversing with Blood, the gentle murmur of the crowd outside had suddenly risen to a cheer. Charles went to the window and was gratified to see an old lady of about seventy endeavouring to climb the area railings. A small boot-boy was standing guard with a broom, and the two were evidently engaged in a verbal interchange which was being cheered by the crowd.

"I can never decide whether a Roman collar gets dirty quicker or slower than an ordinary collar," the parson was saying.

The old lady's bonnet had been knocked off, and Charles was too engrossed to reply.

Suddenly he heard a strangled moan in the room behind him. He turned. Blood's face had turned completely white; his eyes were destitute of expression. He was staring ahead unseeingly. In one hand he held the lid of the laundry basket and in the other a collar. Replacing the lid on the basket, but still holding the collar in his hand, he staggered back to his chair and collapsed into it.

"Good heavens, Blood," said Charles, "what's the matter?"

For two minutes Blood said nothing, but stared at Charles. Twice he made as if to speak, but seemed unable to articulate the words. Slowly the colour drained back to his face.

"Just a touch of faintness," he said painfully at last.

"Look here," Charles said anxiously, "don't you think I had better get a doctor?"

"No," the other answered tonelessly. "I've had these attacks before." He paused. "I once got a go of fever from my bacteriological work and I'm subject to faintness occasionally as the result. I shall be quite all right in a few hours' time. I have some medicine I keep by me."

There was a knock at the door, and Mr Budge appeared. "Come to collect your laundry, sir," he said. "We're a bit short-handed this week, so I'm helping collect the baskets."

Blood's nerves were obviously overwrought as a result of his seizure for he jumped visibly.

"Come again later, Mr Budge," he said in an irritated voice. "Mine isn't ready yet."

"All right, sir," replied Mr Budge, "I'll collect what you've got, and call for the rest later."

If, in Blood's last remark, Charles had detected the twang of overstrung nerves, he now heard a distinct snap.

Blood jumped to his feet and bore down on Budge. "Is this an hotel, or is it a blasted workhouse?" he screamed, with a falsetto quiver in his voice. "Get out of my room; get out of my room at once. Damn and blast you. If I see your bloody face round this door again to-day I'll knock it off."

Charles prepared to act the rôle of the friend who separates two combatants—a task almost as exacting and embarrassing as breaking up a dog-fight; but Mr Budge showed none of the resentment that he would, thought Charles, have been more than human not to show. On the contrary, he retreated with a bland and understanding smile.

"Oh, well, sir, if you feel like that I'm quite prepared to leave your laundry. This disappearance has upset us all."

Before he closed the door, however, he hesitated. "I'm afraid you'll be disturbed again to-day, however. The police are going to search the hotel this evening." Then he was gone.

"I'm sorry, Venables," remarked the parson in a small voice. "My nerves are absolutely in pieces. I don't expect I shall be able to prepare a microscopic slide for three days. You'd better leave me before I make another scene. So long."

Venables left the room, and the parson put the breakfast tray outside, locking the door behind him. He lifted the house telephone and gave instructions that he would be working all the morning and must not be disturbed.

For half an hour he sat in his chair with his head in his hands. For close on another half-hour he paced the room. Then with a gesture in which determination and resignation were equally mingled, he pulled a table into the middle of the room and cleared the top. Drawing on a thin pair of gloves, he went to a cupboard and took out a case of shining instruments.

Then the Rev. Septimus Blood went to the laundry basket and lifted the lid…

III

Bailey tapped his pipe reflectively on the desk. "What do you make of it, Venables?" he said at length. "Is it a real story or isn't it?"

Charles, summoned to report on the Garden Hotel Mystery, nibbled the top of his umbrella. "Difficult to say. Most of these disappearances are disappointing. Unless a corpse turns up somewhere, there's nothing in it. I've got a hunch, though, that something's behind this business that isn't obvious to the eye. There's someone lying like hell, I'm certain, and there's something simmering below the surface at that place that will come to the top sooner or later."

Bailey looked at him keenly. He was an old hand at his game, and more raw material in the shape of journalists had passed through his hands than of anyone else in Fleet Street. He was puzzled now.

"Are you sure you can run this story, Venables?" he asked. "Your first story was excellent, but can you keep it up? To be perfectly frank, you have had no experience of this sort of thing. You were only on the reportorial staff for three months and then you were put on to the gossip column, you know."

"I think I can hold it down all right," answered Charles. "I have one or two lines I should like to work on, and I don't think I will let the *Mercury* down."

"Go ahead then," said the other. "Don't get yourself arrested, and don't let us in for a libel action. Otherwise you'll get all the rope you need. I may say the Chief was extremely keen on your continuing with this assignment. He's a friend of the family, I believe, and he hinted that your murky past qualified you for this."

"Oxford, Geneva and the League of Nations, and rural Surrey, are the extent of my experiences," said Charles innocently. "However, I'll do my best. By the way, I was thinking of leaving the Garden Hotel."

Bailey stared at him. "What! Why on earth..."

"But now," added Charles ingenuously, "I shall stay on."

"Very neat," Bailey acknowledged, smiling. "I, of course, press you to stay there, and you therefore put down your bill at the hotel as part of your expenses. Right oh, carry on; charge it out." In his time Bailey's expenses sheets had been the admiration of Fleet Street.

Charles looked in at Pouncefoot before he left. "Gr-rr—" he said, "I'm fed up with Desirée already. Can't you give her a rest? Put in a paragraph about the new crime specialist of the *Mercury*."

"Who's that?" asked Pouncefoot.

"Me," replied Charles.

IV

Charles might not have been quite so cheerful if he could have seen what was happening in his room.

Kneeling on the floor before his trunk was Eppoliki. With an occasional furtive glance behind him, Eppoliki went steadily through his belongings. Every paper was sorted and examined.

Apparently the results of his search disappointed him. He turned his attention to the chest of drawers, but here again he drew blank.

"Funny," he muttered. "Can he have been telling the truth?" This last proposition seemed too fantastic an assumption for the Egyptian, however, for he resumed his methodical search.

At last he ended his labours. Evidently what he had been searching for was not to be found...

V

The Rev. Septimus Blood hurried down the corridor of the hotel. He glanced stealthily to the left and the right. In his hand he held the battered leather case, bigger than the traditional doctor's bag, which, he had once confided, sometimes contained enough bacilli to wipe out the population of London. At first the residents of the hotel had regarded it with alarm and had shied away from it with the same instinctive shrinking that the normal person exhibits towards an infernal machine. After a time, however, they had become used to it, for it appeared to be his constant companion. "Blood and his little pets," the combination had been nicknamed.

The lounge seemed to be empty. He glanced round. A large vase on the mantelshelf caught his eye.

"Excellent," he mumbled. "Ideal." He opened his bag...

The Rev. Septimus Blood looked round the lobby. Mrs Salterton-Deeley's hat and coat hung on a peg: and below it was a leather hat-case.

Evidently some humorous thought had struck the Rev. Septimus Blood. His lips were parted in a smile. "Hussy," he said to himself, "impudent creature!"

The hat from the hat-box was put in his bag...

VI

A few of the residents were sitting in Mr Budge's own office, on the ground floor, where the dark secrets of his laundry business were discussed and settled.

There was a show-case, glazed, of dress shirts whose gleaming whiteness was in striking contrast to the dusty appearance of the laundry as a whole. Two mottoes, prepared by the United Kingdom Society of Launderers, hung on the wall. "A firmly sewn button cannot come off," said one. "Bad material is shown up by the wash," admonished the other. These two mottoes at once produced an inferiority complex in those who had come to complain about the ravages of Budge's Hand Laundry.

Mr Budge cleared his throat. "Ladies and gentlemen," he said, "no doubt you will wish to know what is to happen to the hotel in my wife's absence—which we all hope is temporary."

"Hear, hear," interjected Mr Winterton, with an adenoidal click.

"I am happy to say that I am temporarily taking my wife's place, and everything will be carried on just as it was in her time... Everything," he repeated with a deep significance that apparently was not lost on his audience.

"That's a great relief for us all," pronounced the Colonel solemnly. "We all felt sure that you could do no less—very worrying all the same."

"Hear, hear," clicked Mr Winterton.

VII

"It's a puzzling case this," Sergeant Noakes advised his wife. "There are times when all sorts of causes of disappearances suggest themselves. Generally, too, the people concerned in the case—relatives or friends—have a pretty shrewd idea of where and why the dear one has legged it."

He shook his head. "It's quite different in this case. Here's a woman ill in bed—reason one why she shouldn't get up and go. And don't suggest that she was shamming," he said menacingly to his wife, who, placidly hemming a sheet at her sewing-machine, hardly looked as if she had any intention of doing so. "I've had that out with the doctor and he said she couldn't possibly be shamming. Not that I trust these experts anyway," he added on a note of despair.

"Point number two," he continued. "I'm perfectly certain that no one in the hotel has the least idea where she's gone to. That damned journalist fellow—a silly ass of a chap—walks round looking as if he knows a lot, and writes up all sorts of daft theories in his rag; but he doesn't know. Now you're going to tell me that the husband knows something." Noakes wagged a finger at his wife. "And so he does, but he doesn't know where she's gone to, I'll be bound."

Mrs Noakes finished her hem. "Why don't you dig up the garden?" she suggested.

"Bah!" Noakes exclaimed disgustedly.

Once, in a case with which he had been connected, his wife had suggested that the body had been buried in the garden. It had been; and the triumph had gone to her head. Ever since she had been unable to make any contribution to any of his cases beyond the suggestion that the body or stolen article had been buried in the garden.

"I wouldn't trust that little one-eyed Egyptian farther than I could throw him," stated the Sergeant, with Anglo-Saxon prejudice.

VIII

Eppoliki gently opened the door of Budge's room. Budge, his back to the door, spun round, and the Egyptian found himself staring into the shaking barrel of an automatic.

Budge dropped it and grinned sheepishly. "God, you startled me," he said. "I've been a bundle of nerves ever since yesterday evening. Did you find anything to bear out your theory?"

The medical student shook his head. "Nothing. Think probably I am wrong. Often am, so they tell me at King's College." He shrugged his shoulders resignedly.

Budge meditated for a space. "No, it's not him, I'm sure. It's some relation of the woman's," he muttered. He didn't use the word "woman" but that was what he meant. "I was a fool, I suppose; but I'm paying for it now. I jump every time anyone comes near me; but they won't have an easy job to get me."

"What's this?" asked the Egyptian, his eyes bright and bird-like with curiosity. "Who you been offending and how?"

Indignation blazed in Budge's eyes and then died out. "Never you mind," he said. "You'll probably know sooner or later."

He dropped the revolver and drummed on the desk with his fingers. His forehead was still damp with the sweat of fear from his first fright when Eppoliki had entered the room so noiselessly. His Adam's apple fluttered as he swallowed.

"The police suspect me," he whispered. "That fellow Noakes keeps asking me silly questions. Polite enough to me, of course, but questions that as good as ask me if I did it."

"Did you?" asked the Egyptian innocently. "You know I'm beginning to wonder whether—"

"I suppose you're trying to be funny," growled the other. "Well, don't, see. You're not."

Chapter Six

HERE WE ARE AGAIN

I t was strange how cordially the suggestion was received.

Seated on a sofa by the fire, Venables, for Viola's benefit, had gradually eliminated the various possibilities.

"So you see the event could never have taken place at all. What fools we mortals be!"

"…admirable fellows and eventually get their man," had droned the Colonel remorselessly nearby. Sergeant Noakes had tactfully complimented him on his handling of the affair, and the old warrior's heart was evidently in cordial sympathy with the police. "Believe me, Mrs Walton," he had gone on, "Scotland Yard never lets up. It may take weeks—it may take years, but sooner or later they get him."

"Nonsense," interjected Miss Mumby. "Clumsy idiots, that's what they are. Socrates went up to speak to that Sergeant Noakes and the brute trod on his foot."

Socrates' ears twitched at the mention of his name, but he kept his eyes fixed on the ball of bright-scarlet wool which unrolled itself with fascinating little jerks and bounds at his mistress's feet as the shapeless scarlet garment on which she was engaged slowly grew.

"And his language," continued Miss Mumby. "Disgraceful, all that fuss over a little scratch. I wrote to the Commissioner protesting about it!"

"Russian gold," explained Mr Winterton. "The country is rotten with it. Look at Invergordon. Look at Dartmoor. Look at the number of murders that take place every year. These fellows stop at absolutely nothing." He dissolved in a staccato series of clicks, expressing his horror of the national situation. "National Party," he muttered darkly. "I could tell you a thing or two about the National Party!"

"Oh, but surely it's saved the country, Mr Winterton," said Miss Geranium. "I read it only the other day in the *Mercury*."

"The *Mercury*! I could tell you something about the *Mercury* too," answered Winterton.

Miss Hectoring looked at him icily. "My father took the *Mercury* from the day it was started," she said. "He was a friend of the proprietor, and often used to discuss its policy with him. 'Camilla,' he said to me shortly before he died, 'if ever they give votes for women, don't trust your own judgment. Do what the *Mercury* tells you!' I have done so ever since." There was a tone of finality in Miss Hectoring's voice, and Winterton contented himself with one noisy suck at a hollow tooth by way of reply, not the least unpleasant of his mannerisms.

It was eleven o'clock and the majority of the residents who did not go to work had, as if by a pre-concerted arrangement, drifted into the lounge. All of them had been seeking information about what was the only possible topic of conversation in the hotel that day. No one fancied the idea of leaving the hotel except Mrs Salterton-Deeley, who was determined to go to the little recherché hat shop she ran in Bond Street even if it meant braving the united stare of the sight-seeing London public still congregated round the Garden Hotel. In fact, being red-headed by nature as well as by art, this prospect added to her determination rather than the reverse.

The residents had soon found that nothing was to be gained by wandering aimlessly round and crudely interrogating the hotel staff and the policemen. They had thus congregated at intervals in the lounge to discuss with never-diminished interest the events of the day.

The suggestion had come in the first place from Miss Mumby. Its cordial reception was due in part to the fact that the company were becoming exceedingly bored with each other. Any suggestion for concerted action would have met with a ready response. And deep down in everyone there is a strain of the primitive, immediate successor to the animism of childhood, and almost as old, which never allows logic and reason and science to extirpate completely the belief in something more than natural, in something uneasy, unexpected, the thirteenth chance, the spilt salt, hybris, the warnings and phantasms of midnight...

"I feel we ought to try to get in touch with Mrs Budge," said Miss Mumby. "Here we are, gathered together," she went on brightly, "with ample spiritual horse-power, as a dear and very wise friend of mine calls it. I feel certain that if we all tried hard and put our *hearts* into it, we could get into touch with the unfortunate woman. At least we could be certain of getting a message of consolation to her, and there is every possibility of getting a message back again, to tell us whereabouts she is.

"In principle," Miss Mumby explained, "the séance will be telepathic. I am assuming that Mrs Budge is incarcerated somewhere and is endeavouring to communicate with us. That task will be rendered simple if we unite our spiritual forces and empty our minds. It may be that Mrs Budge's astral body will enter this room. On the other hand, it may be that one of us will find a message enter his or her mind.

"There is a distinct possibility," she added, "that some kindly spirit may also be attracted to our circle, and supply us with the information which we need, and perhaps give us some consoling message for Mr Budge."

"I don't believe in it," remarked Cantrip gruffly. "Was in India for twenty years and couldn't find a man to do the Indian rope trick."

"This isn't a conjuring trick, Colonel," answered Miss Mumby. "This is a scientific experiment. None knows better than I we may get no result." She shrugged her shoulders. "On the other hand, one sometimes gets amazing results."

"Something in that," admitted the Colonel. "I remember in India seeing a fakir take a red-hot coal in his hand and rub it all over his naked body. Damned hot coal it was, too. It set fire to a piece of paper when I applied it."

"I think it is worth trying," urged Winterton. "I don't believe in it myself, but it can do no harm."

"Oh, do let's try it," exclaimed Mrs Walton. "I have known some wonderful things happen at a séance."

An excellent idea, thought Charles. The Unconscious, given complete liberty of action in a dark room, might play some revealing pranks. He hurriedly tried to recall what he knew of Freudian symbolism.

Under Miss Mumby's directions a light bamboo table was placed in the centre of the lounge. The blinds were drawn and the curtains pulled across. With fingers touching, the ring of adults sat round the table and waited.

In the faint light filtering through the curtains Viola could make out the features of the sitters. Miss Mumby, with grey hair tightly drawn back from her gaunt Scotch face, looked like a sibyl on her tripod waiting for the descent of the prophetic fire. The others had an expression suitable for Church during the course of a long sermon, except for Charles, whose face seemed absolutely devoid of any expression except for a faint sparkle of animation from his monocle.

The heavy silence was broken only by a creak of chairs and a steady wheeze ending with an abrupt click from Mr Winterton, an exaggerated version of which made his table manners so distressing. Eventually it even got on Miss Mumby's nerves.

"Perhaps it will distract our minds," she said, "if we repeat some simple saying. Try this, for instance. *There's so much good in the worst of us and so much bad in the best of us that it ill behoves the most of us to say any ill of the rest of us."*

With a little prompting the seven were soon able to repeat the rigmarole word perfect, and presently a dreary monotone was established which lulled the senses into stupor. Moreover, it had the wanted effect. The table quivered like a high-spirited horse and then started to rock determinedly.

In a voice blank of all feeling Miss Mumby addressed it. "Are you a Good Spirit? Knock once for yes and twice for no."

The table rose and fell once and then was still, shivering slightly. It was a good spirit.

"Are you Mrs Budge?" Miss Mumby asked next, without any preliminary skirmishing.

One knock.

Charles heard a swift intake of breath from Mrs Walton. Miss Geranium's eyes glittered strangely in the twilight. "Sees visions," thought Charles, remembering Viola's words, and was disturbed. Her outburst shortly before had been something more than hysteria.

Colonel Cantrip snorted, but whether in scepticism or surprise, Charles could not make out.

"Where are you?" asked Miss Mumby, the faintest tinge of excitement creeping into her voice. "I shall spell out the alphabet. Please knock once when I reach the required letter, and I will begin again."

"H" spelt the table.

"E"

"L"

"Hell," said the Colonel tactlessly. "It can't be a good spirit."

Miss Geranium half rose to speak and then sat down abruptly.

The table did an abrupt pirouette, and all hurriedly removed their hands for a moment. It sank into quiescence.

There was a shake in Miss Mumby's voice as she went through the alphabet again. She lingered for a moment at "L." The table quivered, but made no movement. "M, N, O, P." The table selected "P" with a decided rap.

"Help," said the Colonel in a surprised tone. "I thought it was going to be 'Hell.'"

The table still shuddered, and in spite of every question that Miss Mumby addressed to it, it was inexorable in its demands for "Help." Efforts to obtain further information from it only appeared to goad it to fury, and it started an insistent rocking which worked up to a stationary dance. This was too much for the nerves of Socrates, who had been sitting quietly by his mistress, and with a miaow of protest he went berserk, tearing round and round the room and leaping on and off chairs and tables. There was a sudden crash as a large Chinese vase on the mantelshelf was whisked off, and the noise seemed to appal even the spirit or, more strictly speaking, the astral body, of Mrs Budge, for the table stopped and went completely dead.

Socrates, pacified by the cessation of the noise, began sniffing in the ruins of the vase. Something had evidently been in it, for he dragged out and carried to Miss Mumby an object which in the uncertain light dimly resembled a glove.

Miss Mumby bent to pick it up. As she did so, to the consternation of everyone, a piercing shriek, of an intensity which Charles had never believed within the scope of a human voice, made Socrates leap very nearly to the ceiling, and sent a chill down the spine of every listener.

II

"Well, Sergeant," remarked Miss Sanctuary, who was sitting on the sofa in the little sitting-room on the ground floor which was her pet retreat, "have you discovered any trace of Mrs Budge, or of the person who attacked me?"

"None at all," groaned the Sergeant. "It is a most puzzling case. Here is Mrs Budge completely disappeared; so far as we can see she can't have vanished voluntarily, and yet our organization, which is, as you know, pretty thorough, cannot pick up a trace of her. Not the tiniest, remotest trace," he added, carefully inspecting the inside of his helmet as if looking for the trace.

Miss Sanctuary was silent for a moment. She looked up from the scarf she was knitting and glanced at him shrewdly. "I know nothing about these things beyond the detective stories I read," she said, smiling, "but I can't help imagining that a little research into the Budges' past might help a little."

The Sergeant returned her glance by one equally penetrating. He had already sized her up as a knowing old lady, for all her benevolent mien—he had an aunt who was the very spit of her, and as cunning as a cart-load of monkeys.

"You're right, madam, that would be the obvious line of inquiry, if we had a real case," he answered. "But, you see, it isn't a crime to disappear. We have been called in in the first place by Mr Budge to help him find his wife. We cross-examine him certainly, and he gives us all the information he has, or"—the Sergeant looked knowing—"all the information he thinks it good for us to have. That's all. I haven't really any right to be here talking to you in this hotel except that Mr Budge has asked us in to help him."

"I see your point, Sergeant," answered Miss Sanctuary. "But

what about the attack on me? I may be egotistical, but isn't that important enough to justify the police taking a strong line?"

The Sergeant thought long and deeply. "It is and it isn't," he answered guardedly at last. "It all depends on the motive which caused the man to attack you. It wasn't robbery, so far as we know, and it must be connected with the disappearance of Mrs Budge. So back we come to the disappearance. If it were the ordinary robbery with violence case it would be easy. Who are the known criminals of the type out of prison, and where were they at the time in question? Those would be the lines we should go on—a mere routine job, you see! But here's something different. There's nothing to give us a line on who it is. Once we know what really happened, then we've something to start from. At present it's a complete fog."

"I think I see what you mean," replied Miss Sanctuary. "You want a clue, and it may not be a material clue—a dropped cigarette or a finger-print—it may be just a motive, an indication of the type of mind of the criminal which will provide you with the end of a thread which you can grasp and follow to its termination."

"That's it," admitted the Sergeant. He crossed his knees and looked coldly at the inside of his helmet, in which there was still apparently no trace of Mrs Budge. "Of course if only we knew one way or the other. Supposing it was *murder*, for instance"—he dropped his voice gloatingly—"then if we knew *that* we should act very differently, I can tell you! We should pull the house to pieces from top to foundations, and we should pull you people to pieces too. As far as the Judges' rules would let us," he added gloomily.

"Of course," he went on, "the case would be taken out of my hands, but I should probably work with the Inspector who was put in charge of the case, and I would get the credit for the preliminary work—or discredit, it might be," he qualified.

Miss Sanctuary affected to shudder. "I hope it isn't murder," she said. "I don't like the enthusiastic way you talk about it, and I don't like the way you talk about pulling us to pieces."

She paused a moment. "I think I can help you a little," she added, "if in return you'll help me."

The Sergeant looked puzzled. "Certainly, I'll help you," he answered.

"Hold out your hands then!"

Mystified, he did so. She deftly placed a skein of wool round them and started rolling it into a ball.

"These are the only times I regret being a spinster," she said. "I haven't even a brother or nephew. It's a perpetual source of astonishment to me that wool manufacturers still sell their wool in skeins. Well, Sergeant, now that you are helpless, I'll tell you something. I've been trying to think of some little point that might help you to identify the person who attacked me. Last night, just as I was going to sleep, I suddenly remembered quite vividly that the hand that was pressed over my mouth had a ring on it. You know how sensitive the skin round one's mouth is, and I remember how painful this ring was, and that it felt as if instead of being a smooth band it was serrated or ornamented in some way, because as the hand was dragged across my face I felt it pull at the skin."

"Which side of your face was the hand?" asked the Sergeant.

"The left," she answered.

"Do you recall what finger the ring would have been on?"

She thought for a moment. "Not the little finger and not the forefinger," she said at last; "either the second or third."

Released from the wool at last, the Sergeant made a note in his book. "Ring with ornamented band on second or third finger," he wrote. "That should help us a little," he said. "If only you can think of some other distinctive feature, do. Remember these small clues are useless except cumulatively."

Miss Sanctuary smiled. "It was all so sudden," she remarked. "I am afraid you must be very annoyed with me for not being able to tell you more."

"Nonsense," he replied. "Far rather you knew nothing than like so many other witnesses, recalled what didn't happen. I must be going now. If my wife had her way, I should be digging up the yard, but as it is, I'm going to see if I can extract some information from Budge—a difficult job, that."

"The man must have made some enemies and so must the woman," the Sergeant thought as he went into Budge's room. "Just the type that does, *I* should say."

III

"So there you are, Sergeant," concluded Budge. "I am afraid I can give you no useful information at all. Have a cigarette?"

He extended his case. The Sergeant, hand in mid-air, paused. On the second finger of the hand holding the case was a golden ring with a band in the form of two plaited serpents interlocked like a chain.

"A pretty ring that," he commented, "and unusual."

"Yes," replied Budge. "I got it—"

But the Sergeant never heard the end of the sentence. "Good heavens!" he exclaimed. "Who is that screaming like a maniac?"

IV

Miss Mumby's scream certainly penetrated to every part of the hotel and probably reached the crowd of sightseers who still lingered round the railings. If it did, however, their attention was already too engrossed by the little drama which was being enacted in front of them, and which was to make the Garden Hotel a name of sinister import all over the world.

Mrs Salterton-Deeley, in order to face the crowd with equanimity, had made efforts to look her best. One of her own hats was perched like a bird of passage on the front left-hand quarter of her red hair. She carried a leather hat-box. She had placed in it the previous evening a hat which she had brought back to the hotel for the purpose of trimming.

With much murmuring and personal comment the crowd made way for her, until some blithe spirit at the back called out to her in fruity cockney, "Hi, miss, are you carrying away the body in that there box?"

This seemed to tickle the crowd, and somebody else shouted, "Show us the body, miss. Be a sport."

Mrs Salterton-Deeley prided herself on the good-humoured *savoir-faire* with which she managed the lower classes. Smiling, she snapped up the catch of the hat-box and opened the lid.

"There you are," she said.

Inside was a severed human head; the head, in fact, of Mrs Budge.

Chapter Seven

DISJECTA MEMBRA

Mrs Salterton-Deeley swooned—there was no other word to describe her immediate prostration upon the pavement. During a shocked second the crowd was silent. For the first time they had had a sudden close-up of the horrors about which they read so eagerly in the papers, which they discussed so absorbedly in restaurants and in trains, and which made them flock, with the sure and swift instinct of carrion-eating birds, to the scene of a crime of violence. The old lady with a bonnet, whose invasion had been successfully repelled by the boot-boy earlier that morning, dissolved in a cackle of metallic laughter, punctuated by great wheezing sobs. Two people went away and were silently and painfully ill.

It seemed hours before anyone made a decisive move. In actual fact it was only three minutes before the policeman, on duty forty yards away, had reached Mrs Salterton-Deeley's side and, aided by the hall-porter, had removed her and her ghastly burden into the hotel. Five minutes later he had found Sergeant Noakes, who was searching for the source of the scream. That officer, shaken out of his habitual calm, had rushed down the stairs two at a time.

The Sergeant's face was grave when he was shown the gruesome relic in the hat-box. It grew even graver when he was shown the severed right hand, which had come to light in such an extraordinary way during the séance in the lounge.

"This ends our period of doubt, at any rate," he said. "Here's murder as plainly as can be. I'll get on to Bray, and have him over as soon as possible."

And while Bray was listening to Noakes's story with surprise and interest intermingled, Charles was on the line to the *Post*, the *Mercury*'s evening paper, giving them a story beside which the morning's "splash" hid its diminished headlines. The *Post* was an hour ahead of its rivals on that historic day, and had the only eye-witness's story of the incredible séance in the lounge of the Garden Hotel, and the effect of the *Mercury*'s follow-up on the British public has already been described.

II

There could be little, if any, doubt as to what might be expected after the almost simultaneous appearance of the head and the hand. The hotel was searched and it was found that with almost fiendish ingenuity the body of the proprietress of the hotel had been severed into handy sizes and disposed in different parts of the hotel, all in hiding-places where immediate discovery was not likely, but where, on the other hand, it would be only a matter of time before at least one of the gruesome relics came to light.

The time of discovery, the place and the receptacle of each portion was carefully noted and the complete remains placed in a small box-room which was turned into a temporary mortuary.

A special late edition of the *Post* was rushed out in honour of the new developments, and Charles spent most of his time visiting the phone to add fresh paragraphs to his story. He was just walking across the hall after giving a last sensational item to be "fudged" in the final edition, when he ran into Bray.

Charles jumped. "Good heavens," he said, "are you the sleuth-hound on this job?"

Detective Inspector Bernard Bray, C.I.D., and Charles Venables were friends, with a friendship dating from the day when Bray, son of the Rev. Timothy Bray in whose parish of Better Gaming the Venables's fast-dwindling estate of Tankards was situated, had been (as a rowing Blue and runner-up for the All-England Pole Jumping Championship) fit object of respect for a youth some five years his junior. Bray was even more surprised to see Venables than Charles was to see him.

"Hello, Charles," he said. "This is a funny place for a society journalist to be in. I'm surprised at Noakes allowing you to wander round here anyway."

"As I happen to be a resident here, you needn't be surprised," answered Charles, "and in addition I happen at the moment to be the *Mercury*'s star crime reporter."

Bray laughed. "You scoffed somewhat when I became a bobby five years ago," he said. "Now you will have to treat me with proper respect as your main source of information."

"You may even have to arrest me," replied Charles. "I have a watertight alibi which is alone enough to fasten suspicion on to me. Add the fact that I only arrived at the hotel yesterday, and I am almost prepared to give myself in charge."

"I'm rather sorry you are on the *Mercury*," said Bray, with an abstracted air, and abruptly changing the subject. "It will somewhat limit your use to me. At any rate do you mind keeping anything interesting you have noticed—and you are a reasonably observant beggar—until my preliminary investigation is complete? Then I'd like a word with you. Cheerio."

"Cheerio," said Charles, and returned to Viola, who looked uncommonly pallid.

III

Because there is nothing to the run of humanity more sacred than life, the *lex talionis*, which is still a motivation of penal systems, gives the policeman even in England unique power and authority in a case of murder. After Mrs Budge had disappeared, the fact, even taken in conjunction with the assault on Miss Sanctuary, only brought in the police as little more than servants in the Garden Hotel, invited by the aggrieved parties to defend and protect them.

Now a blow had been aimed at the safety of society itself. Each uniformed figure, each plain-clothes detective, was now, under heaven's and the Judges' rules, accountable only to society. All the secrets of the lives of the residents of the Garden Hotel would, if necessary, be dragged to light, and no one at that time had any conception of how tangled and tortuous a story there would be to tell...

In the lounge where Charles and Viola were sitting, there was dead silence. It was shattered by the entrance of Miss Geranium, with flushed face and straggling hair.

"I have seen the warning of the Most High," she cried, glaring menacingly at Colonel Cantrip, who was fidgeting in a chair reading a paper, "and the message was *woe to this sinful generation*. Vengeance is the Lord's and the Lord will repay. The finger of the Lord is on us all. First, the tempter then the tempted." She advanced abruptly to the Colonel. "It will be your turn next," she said, pointing with a steady finger at him, "and yours too," she shouted, wheeling round on Miss Mumby, who had just come in, attracted by the noise, "you trifler with the spirits of darkness and evil. And then it will be my turn," she moaned, in a voice thick with despair. "The Lord have mercy on us sinners."

The Colonel jumped to his feet. "How dare you address me in that offensive manner!" he said. "By God, I won't stand it on top of all I've been through. I won't. I won't." And to the amazement of Viola and Charles the military gentleman burst into tears, which he made no attempt to restrain.

Miss Mumby, however, was quite undisturbed by this outburst. She beamed placidly on Miss Geranium, standing like a Hebrew prophet in the full fire of her denunciation, and at Colonel Cantrip, looking like a naughty boy with the tears streaming down his rubicund cheeks.

"Well, well," she said, "we all seem to be a bit under the weather, don't we? Never mind, there's a letter for each of you in your rooms," and she made the last commonplace remark in a voice full of meaning.

It meant something to both her hearers apparently. They went out of the room without any further preamble, Miss Geranium forgetting her denunciation and the Colonel his sorrows.

"I can't stand much more of this, really I can't," said Viola. "I almost sympathize with the Colonel. I said this hotel was weird, and I feel now as if all the weirdness was boiling and working and getting more and more restive. It's like one of those dreadful fireworks that explode once but which go on smoking and fizzing afterwards as if they were going to give a much bigger bang any moment. Now that the police are on the scene one ought to feel that everything is going to be cleared up tidily, but actually I feel as if things are only going to get a good deal more tangled."

"Yes, there is something in the atmosphere like that," said Charles. He went to the door, looked out, and returned. "It affects me, so that I have a creepy feeling every time I speak to anyone alone. I think that's partly the effect of all that's happened in the last twenty-four hours—sudden death, hysterics, goodness knows what. Deep down in me I feel I must get to the bottom of it, and I wouldn't leave here till it is cleared up for a thousand pounds."

"Well, I wouldn't stay for a thousand," replied Viola, "if you weren't here."

Charles sat up and endeavoured to look protective.

"I do know, then," Viola went on seriously, "that with Mrs Walton and Eppoliki we shall have a reasonably sane four for contract, and that's more than can be said of any of the others at the moment."

Charles leaned back again. "Bridge!" he said bitterly.

IV

Bray never formed any conclusion, or ventured any opinion, until every fact that seemed to have a superficial bearing on the case had been assimilated. His passion for facts had been entirely responsible for his brilliant handling of the three cases by which he had made his name. It is doubtful if anyone but Bray could have secured the conviction of Twemling, whose subtle method of bacilli poisoning defeated direct evidence. The sheer weight of details amassed by Bray, each in themselves unconvincing, but damning in the aggregate, had given Sir Lawrence Foederer the ammunition which his clear logic could aim with invincible accuracy.

Now Bray strolled over the Garden Hotel, crawled about the roofs, and committed its general lay-out to mind. He was fond of expounding his technique of investigation with a certain donnish pedantry.

He would explain that criminal investigation was in essence a reconstruction of the crime, and it was a reconstruction in four dimensions—in the space-time continuum. Position in time could be as fatal to a criminal as position in space.

When he had satisfied himself perfectly as to the space-frame of the Garden Hotel murder, then he proceeded to extend it into the fourth dimension. Everyone inside the hotel was interrogated. Sparing of comment, keen of eye, the young detective gradually filled a notebook with the times of the individuals whose geodesics might have crossed the world line of Mrs Budge (so abruptly cut off) at the hour of nine-thirty.

V

White-coated and rubber-gloved, Dr Wuthering straightened himself and turned from the autopsy table.

"Killed round about nine-thirty, but of course after this lapse of time and in this state, I may be four hours out either way. Cause of death due to strangulation. The line of decapitation is below the line of strangulation, and I should say the latter was done with a thin cord, placed round and drawn tight. The body was dissected at least twelve hours after death. It is a good, workmanlike job by someone with anatomical knowledge but not a surgeon. Looks more like a G.P. or medical student."

VI

"Revolting, absolutely revolting," snorted Colonel Cantrip to Miss Mumby. "By gad, I've seen some horrors in India, but I tell you I felt absolutely white about the gills. I don't blame you for screaming." He dragged at his grey moustaches. "I nearly screamed myself."

"What's this, Colonel? Don't scream; please don't scream," implored Mr Nicholas Twing.

Twing was manager of an issuing house in the City. Money seems to have two effects on those who come most intimately into contact with it. Either it plumps their bodies and reddens their cheeks, or it dries them up like parchment. In Mr Twing desiccation had been carried past all reason. He looked like one of those withered heads of Papua, in which the features are perfect, but which some secret process of curing has reduced to only a fraction of full scale. His delicate little hands, with their perfect nails, were like buzzards' talons, and his black, beady eyes looked out of a face seared with the innumerable scorings of a palimpsest half as old as time.

He laid one of his talons on the Colonel's arm now, and his beady eyes probed the Colonel's face. "It wouldn't take much to make you scream after all," he said at length. "Your nerves are in a shocking state, Cantrip."

Cantrip's bloodshot eyes roamed round the room. "Well, can you wonder at it?" he said testily. "It's all very upsetting not knowing from one minute to the next whether one isn't going to disappear and be found in pieces scattered about the place."

Mr Twing laughed shrilly. "It is unsettling, certainly. The way I look at it is this. One of the residents in this place must have done it—oh, don't look so startled; surely that much is obvious even to you! Now, as we meet you in everyday life, not one of you good people seems capable of it. Even our superannuated military friend here"—he indicated Cantrip with a wave of his claws—"has long ago lost the guts for such a deed, if he ever had them. So what does it amount to? One of us here is a maniac, neither more nor less, and probably isn't even aware that he has committed the murder."

Mr Twing's eyes roved brilliantly to Miss Mumby's face. "Trances, séances, visions, an animal crank!" he declared. "All significant, all significant!" He turned suddenly on Cantrip. "And our worthy friend here—with his hob-nailed liver and tendency to apoplexy—we all know the eccentricities of retired military gentlemen with nothing to occupy their minds."

He paused a moment, and joined his slender-boned hands in front of him. "It might have been me; oh, yes, it might have been me," he admitted. "I don't remember doing it, but I can imagine my unconscious self getting quite a lot of pleasure out of strangling someone"—he made a gesture towards Miss Mumby, who shuddered and drew back—"and then slicing them up and putting them here and there."

"Really, Mr Twing, if I took you seriously," retorted Miss Mumby, "I shouldn't care to be alone in the hotel with you."

"And I tell you what I think, Twing," remarked the Colonel heatedly, "and that is that if you go round talking like that in the police's hearing you'll find yourself in the dock before you know where you are. Maniac, indeed! Budge is a sly devil and probably won't admit it, but if you ask me, the fellow who murdered Mrs Budge was after something, and Budge knows what it was. What's more, between you and me and the gatepost, I think he's got it. I don't pretend to be particularly observant, but friend Budge has been dead scared about something to-day."

"Anyway, we've got the police in now," stated Mr Twing with malicious satisfaction, "and here they'll stay until they've either found the murderer or somebody they can convince a jury did the murder. Meanwhile, they'll peer and pry into everyone's private affairs."

He advanced on Miss Mumby and his beady eyes twinkled at her. "Do your private affairs bear investigation?" he asked. "Do the Colonel's? Do mine? Oh, we haven't murdered anyone, or robbed anyone, or blackmailed anyone, but we all have our private weaknesses, our little vices, haven't we? And all of them to be dragged out into the light of day." He lifted his talons in a gesture that was a mockery of despair. "Poor little vices, so kindly and happily tucked away in an hotel in Kensington, and now these brutes of policemen are going to trample all over them with their great clumsy feet!"

Miss Mumby tossed her head. "You needn't try to frighten me, Mr Twing. If anybody ought to be scared I fancy it's you. I am going to give the police all the help I can as a citizen, and so far as it assists to find the solution of this terrible crime. Beyond that I shall not go. If they try to pry into affairs that are no concern of theirs I shall put my foot down."

Miss Mumby folded her arms and looked fiercely at Twing. He divined that putting the foot down would be a formidable and awe-inspiring process in her case.

"An excellent spirit—the true Scots independence," he cackled. "Keep it up—you'll need to. Here's a little prophecy I'm going to make. There'll be another murder in this hotel before we're much older—there's someone walking about now who expects to be the victim, too! Well, well, I must go and do some work now."

Twing shuffled out of the room, but at the door he paused and turned.

"One word of advice, my dear Miss Mumby. Don't wear those black velvet bands round your beautiful white throat. They're too tempting to the Unconscious." He made a strangling gesture with his claws. "Asking for it, absolutely. Even a sane man like myself can hardly resist it!"

The door closed, but they heard his high-pitched cackling as he went down the corridor.

Chapter Eight

A MESSAGE FROM THE VICTIM

The technique of criminal investigation is based on the assumption that the murderer leaves, unlike Theseus, *three* strands which will bring the investigator to the heart of his labyrinth of crime. The three strands together are strong enough to hang him. Bereft of one, the prosecuting counsel can rarely weave a rope strong enough for the hangman's purposes.

The first and obvious is physical ability. A murder occurs between ten and four. Five people only are known to have passed into the house and seen the victim in that time. Which of them is tied to the murder by the other strands of motive and material evidence?

A cherished desire for revenge, an angry quarrel, self-interest— out of these the criminal investigator can spin the second strand, needing only one more to make it a fatal web.

That third strand is the material clue to which the police of this country, probably rightly, give especial prominence. The fingerprint, the revolver purchased a day or two before, the shred of clothing—here is a witness amenable to the direct examination and cross-examination of experts, something to be seen and handled, not quite direct evidence, but partaking of its nature.

Each of these three strands may lead the investigator through innumerable twists and turns of the labyrinth; each may lead him to more than one suspect. With the patience of an institution and the vast resources of bureaucracy, the Yard follows up each one of these avenues, exploring each turning off it—cul-de-sac after cul-de-sac. The most obvious trails are followed first, but as the Yard draws blank it retraces its steps, and the less obvious are pursued. The criminal must have a feeling similar to a fox who has taken refuge from the hounds in a hiding-place from which he can see them draw false trail after trail, only to return to the scent again and pick up another. It is their *métier*; they have nothing else to do, and sooner or later, unless a hundredth chance intervenes, they will pick up the right scent and the hunt will be up.

Bray's first line of approach was that of physical possibility. Was it an outside or an inside job? The subsequent disposal of the corpse pointed most strongly to an inside job. In addition, if it were an outside job, the murderer must have escaped from the house subsequently to the time when the doors were guarded.

It transpired that during the quarter of an hour before the doors were guarded, there had been at least one servant near them who would certainly have noticed a stranger. The times did not make an earlier escape remotely feasible.

It was possible that the murderer had escaped by one of the windows. Bray could hardly believe he would have attempted this in a brightly lit and fairly crowded street. While he was verifying the alibis of the household, he came upon evidence which disposed of an exit from windows at the back.

Kitty Higgins, a chambermaid, was somewhat confused when she was asked as to where she had been between nine and ten. She stated that it was her afternoon off, but Bray pressed her and soon extracted from her the fact that between those times she had been giving a lingering farewell at the back door to the baker's roundsman, her companion of the evening. They had glanced up several times at the windows of the house to see that they were not overlooked, and Bray felt in the circumstances that, at any rate, as an initial simplification, he would eliminate an outside job.

This left only the inmates of the hotel at the time of the murder as possibilities, and the bulk of these were soon weeded out. All the hotel staff during that hour were able to give convincing alibis for each other. The nurse was vouched for by the fact that Miss Sanctuary was talking to her at the moment of her assault, and there was a cast-iron alibi for Eppoliki, Colonel Cantrip, Mrs Walton, Venables and Lady Viola Merritt.

Miss Geranium and Miss Hectoring were brewing a final night-cap of malted milk at the time. Mr Winterton, Mr Twing, Mr Blood, Mrs Salterton-Deeley and Miss Mumby, however, were each in their rooms from eight till ten, and these were provisionally marked as possible suspects.

Therefore after his first rough preliminary investigation, Bray was left with six suspects as a nucleus for further investigation, those residents whose movements were unaccounted for at the time, and Mr Budge.

Mr Budge was an object of prime suspicion because there was definite evidence that he was on the scene of the murder at or about the time of its commission. The other three were secondary suspects inasmuch that none of them could produce any proof of the fact that they were in their rooms at the time. Needless to say, at this stage of the investigation, Bray could not personally interrogate them beyond obtaining a bare statement of their whereabouts, but he could, and did, find out indirectly from the other residents and members of the staff that any one of them could have left his or her room, gone in the adjoining bedroom, climbed over the balcony into Mrs Budge's room and returned again without being seen. It would need luck and careful timing, but it could be done. He traced various possible movements of the characters on the large plans he had drawn up, and came to the conclusion that it was physically possible for any of his four suspects, or even two working in conjunction, to have performed the murder.

He also put it down as a working hypothesis that Miss Sanctuary might have been an accessory before the fact. It would have made the murderer's task very much easier had Miss Sanctuary been expecting him, and the assault and tying up might easily have been staged to divert suspicion.

Although this hypothesis had to be admitted as a possibility, Bray realized it would be useless unless he could discover some motive linking Miss Sanctuary with the murderer or the victim.

His more immediate problem was to link one of the suspects themselves to the crime, either by a material clue or a motive. Experience told him that apart from crimes of sudden anger, or of passion, the motives of a crime are all financial. Financial transactions are almost inseparable from documentary evidence, and he therefore spent half an hour going through Mrs Budge's desk.

Mrs Budge had an orderly mind. All the business of documents inseparable to the running of even such a small affair as the Garden Hotel were docketed. Her cash-book and other books of account were posted up to date, although the private ledger was missing. Her business correspondence was filed in a simple letter-file.

Mr Budge's desk, which Bray took the liberty of going through without previously asking permission, was equally businesslike. The laundry business, Bray gathered from a glance through the private ledger, did not do much more than pay its way. Yet of personal correspondence there was not a trace, not even a letter from a friend.

Bray felt that this fact in itself was significant. A person who either has no friends or destroys all personal correspondence is an odd creature and demands investigation. So leaving Sergeant Billings and his myrmidons to complete their methodical search for the material clue—a task at which they were, he recognized, more competent than he was himself—he decided to go round to the firm of solicitors whose address he had found among Mrs Budge's papers.

I I

The room of the proprietor of the *Mercury* who, in conformity with the Northcliffe tradition was always spoken of by his staff as "the Chief," is known, at least by repute, to everyone in Fleet Street. It is situated on the top floor of the glittering lemon-yellow and gilt building which houses the *Mercury* and its satellite "evening," and from its window can be seen the smoky vista of South London with, on sunny days, the Crystal Palace sparkling in the distance like a shining angel guarding the entrance to the Garden of Eden of the Surrey countryside beyond.

The room is completely square, with a plain oak floor, destitute of covering, and with ceiling and walls plainly distempered in a lighter shade of the lemon-yellow which makes the *Mercury* façade so unique. The sliding door is flush with the walls and virtually concealed, and the room is lighted by panels in the ceiling. The Chief's desk is a plain, massive structure, and never, in the history of the *Mercury*, has it had more than one document on it, and that document the one the Chief happened to be dealing with at the time.

The only other articles of furniture in the room, beside the Chief's chair, are five plain oak chairs disposed symmetrically round the desk and screwed to the floor.

There is apparently no telephone. Flush with the desk is a grille concealing the diaphragm of a dictograph, and through the meshes have come at various times the voices of a President speaking from America, a Prime Minister from Chequers, a King from Cannes, and a celebrated assassin threatening vengeance from a remote South American Republic. Leaning back in his chair, with the pose that Sir Evan Pouter, R.A., has made familiar, the Chief had gazed unwinkingly at the Crystal Palace and answered each with the same mellow suavity that had made a tortured old bull of a politician, with a dozen of the *Mercury*'s darts sticking in his hide, describe him at a public meeting as "the slimiest old devil in Christendom."

Well, the Chief at any rate had inherited a great tradition. A newspaper was not for him a mere vehicle for profit, whereby the Pelion of debentures might be piled on the Ossa of equity. First and foremost (at how many journalists' functions had the mellow voice repeated this phrase!) he was a working journalist. It was his pride to return from some great banquet or spectacle at which he had been an honoured guest, and write out a report of it in his meticulous rounded hand. The sub who knew his Chief did not hesitate to slash it to ribbons and put it in finally as a three-line paragraph.

Even Charles, whose imperturbability was the most cherished feature of his existence, felt a little nervous when he sat in the chair reserved for friends in the Chief's room. What was the *Mercury*, he asked himself? A paper that by pandering to the basest sensationalism of the common people climbed on stepping-stones of discarded ethics to higher things. A paper whose public had brains with linings so corroded and crusted by jazz, sentimental films and cheap literature that the most earth-shaking events of the world had to be predigested and peptonized before they could be absorbed. A paper whose political policy had been invariably allied with the most reactionary and antisocial elements of English life. A paper whose tip for the Derby had never once come off…

Yet a paper where power one could feel, like a Shekinah glory, reflected on the faces with which, as a representative of the paper, one came into contact. Politicians, suavely longing for the *Mercury*'s endorsement, actresses yearning with big eyes at the *Mercury*'s reporter, bishops oilily congratulating the power of the press, press agents craven with desire for a "front-page story." And here, in the Holy of holies as it were, was this power incarnate—the Chief.

"I think I know more about you, as a friend of the family, than anyone in the building," the Chief was saying. "That's why I pressed for you to be put on this assignment. Are you going to justify my confidence in you?"

Charles was examining his gloves assiduously. "Have my stories been all right up to the present?" he asked.

"Oh, excellent, my dear boy, excellent. As a working journalist, I congratulate you. As the editor of this paper, I want something more." He paused.

"Now we are getting down to brass tacks at last," thought Charles.

"Anyone can report a matter of this kind, if they were in your position and were competent journalists." The Chief had been speaking to Charles as if to his dictograph. Now he shot a glance at him which Charles parried, or at any rate palliated, as best he could with his monocle. "You're in a privileged position. You've got brains. Find out who really murdered Mrs Budge, or at any rate find some material clue before the police do, so that the *Mercury* can get the credit—so that whenever we write about a crime in future, our public will think of us as the paper that was cleverer than the police." He waved away the incipient remonstrance that was agitating Charles. "Oh, I know what you are going to say—how papers have had to drop the special crime investigator because of the law of libel and because they obstructed the police. Well, you mustn't be libellous and you mustn't obstruct the police—Bray's a friend of yours, by the way, isn't he? I remember seeing him at Tankards—but beat the police on this crime, just this once, and the *Mercury*'s made for at least ten years—an authority on every and any case without another stroke of investigation."

"I'll do my best," said Charles humbly. It didn't sound very impressive, but it was all he could think of at the moment. Sitting in one room with the Chief, one felt as if there wasn't really room for one, as if one was being overcrowded, pressed against the wall by his abundant personality.

"What's your own opinion of the case at this stage?" the Chief had asked.

"I have a theory so fantastic that at present I would rather file it at the back of my head and proceed along ordinary lines," answered Charles. "'Ordinary lines' are these. Certain people could have done the murder. Who? Check up their alibis. It's all part of a routine job. Certain people could have cut up the body and disposed of it. Who? Check up their alibis. If only one person is in both groups, he is the murderer."

"But is he?" said the Chief. "I used to be quite good at Logic at Oxford, and I should say that the deduction only was logical, given that the murderer and the person who disposed of the body were one and the same person."

"That's so," admitted Charles. "They may be different people. If so, God help us! The case is going to be so infernally tangled that it passes my comprehension how it will ever be solved. In that case, we shall be reduced to motive. Why kill Mrs Budge, poor, harmless creature of a proprietress doing an efficient job in an efficient way?

"There may be no motive, of course. It may be the work of a maniac. If one applied William of Occam's razor and refused to multiply entities, the hypothesis of a maniac would be the easiest way out. It would allow for every discrepancy, however irrational, because a maniac cannot be expected to be rational. But I distrust that theory on principle. I'm going to act on the assumption that the murderer's very much cleverer than I am, and that nothing is done without a cause.

"The most disquieting feature of the case is that Budge sticks out about a mile as the murderer. I happen to know there was bad blood between the two. If he is the murderer, then the *Mercury* hasn't a look-in because everything will fall into the police's lap like ripe apples. I am clinging to the belief that Budge is an intelligent fellow. He is quite capable of murdering somebody, but if he did, he would have a damn good alibi. But so far as I can see, he's got no alibi at all."

"Crime has always interested me," commented the Chief. "I would like to tell you, for what it is worth, a theory of mine formed as a result of my study. I think that the criminal betrays himself not in the carefully planned deed itself, when action cools his nerve and clears his brain, but afterwards when anxiety—perhaps even remorse—conjures up phantoms that plague him. The callow criminal returns anxiously to the scene of the murder: in more subtle brains the unrest takes the form of more work put into covering up the tracks—a consolidation of the alibi, an elimination of witnesses who might be hostile. Therefore if the police's preliminary investigation reveals nothing, wait for the false step subsequently that will put you on the trail."

The Chief's voice died away. Sharp and clear, the voices of newsboys with the latest evening edition rose from the street. Traffic drifted soundlessly down the distant river, and the setting sun conjured the Crystal Palace into topaz.

III

"I've seen the papers, of course," said Mr Tarr, reaching out for a box of cigarettes, and then changing his mind and unearthing a cigar. "Naturally I was expecting you."

Messrs Tarr, Waters & Tarr of Bedford Row were not the cobwebbed attorneys of fiction. Bray found himself in offices whose rubber flooring and wealth of new oak panelling suggested a bank, and the rosy-gilled, prosperous-looking solicitor who saw him was very much the man of the world. Perhaps a little too consciously so, but it was a very convincing performance.

"I take it you are Mrs Budge's family solicitor?" suggested Bray.

"Not quite the family solicitor of legend," smiled the lawyer. "Mrs Budge was one of our most valued clients, but we know extremely little about her personal affairs, and nothing of her previous history before she walked into our office five years ago."

"She was not introduced to you?" queried Bray.

"No," replied Tarr. He removed his pince-nez and polished them abstractedly. He appeared to be measuring his words. "As a firm we have traditions, but we pride ourselves, Inspector, on being in touch with the times. The day of the aristocracy has passed. We poor professional devils must bow the knee to plutocracy." (Bray visioned him, pink and embarrassed, bowing the knee.) "By that standard Mrs Budge needed neither references nor introductions."

"Evidently he had suspicions about the good lady," thought the Inspector. Aloud he said, "That suggests a new line of thought. What approximately would Mrs Budge be worth?"

Tarr hesitated. "Naturally I am not prepared to name any definite figure. I could, I think, state a minimum, but the estate may have debts of which I know nothing. I should say Mrs Budge would cut up for—h'm, perhaps the phrase is rather unfortunate—I should say the estate could not conceivably be less than £50,000—possibly nearer £100,000."

"Good heavens!" exclaimed Bray. "This is far beyond what one could imagine. How was this fortune made?"

"I have never seen the Garden Hotel," answered the lawyer, surprised at the policeman's surprise, "but it was evidently a very paying proposition. I suppose it was some great white-tiled barn of a place, and I know both my client and her husband lived very simply."

"The Garden Hotel is in effect a small Kensington boarding-house," retorted Bray. "At the moment it has twelve guests, and I should say its maximum capacity is twenty."

It was Tarr's turn to be surprised. "Good gracious," he said, "I find this almost incredible. Mrs Budge was able to put by over £10,000 a year, and I have always assumed it was the profit from the hotel."

"Well, you can take it quite definitely that it isn't," retorted Bray, and was pleased to see the lawyer look disturbed. "How can I find out the source of this profit?"

"I suggest you see Vernon, her bank manager, who will give you every help he can. I warn you, however, that he may not be able to help you, since I know that, like myself, he is under the impression that Mrs Budge's money was all made from the Garden Hotel."

"I will get Samuel to go over and see him," said Bray. "He is an experienced accountant, and I back him to find out where every penny of Mrs Budge's money emanates from. Meanwhile I should like to ask you a question. Have you any reason to believe that Mrs Budge had any enemies?"

The lawyer thought a moment. "Until the day before her murder I should have said 'No,'" he replied. "An event took place on that day which leads me to modify my reply as far as to say that Mrs Budge may conceivably have had some reason for fear."

The detective was all attention.

"Mrs Budge came into my office and said that she wished to execute a will, as she did not wish to die intestate and leave her husband unprovided for. While agreeing with her in principle, I pointed out that in any event, should she die intestate, her husband would inherit, as she was without issue. She insisted on a will being made there and then, in which she devised all her property, real and personal, to her husband. The original phrasing of my pencilled draft was 'to my husband, George Edward Budge,' but she insisted on crossing out the words 'my husband.'" The lawyer paused as if expecting a comment.

"From which one might deduce that in the eyes of the law, George Edward Budge would be a more accurate description than 'my husband.'"

"Exactly," said the lawyer, pleased that his point had been taken without his committing himself. "Naturally, I made no comment, since such a state of affairs is not uncommon in one's practice. Now, when she had signed the will and seen it witnessed, she made a remark which, in the light of after events, seems profoundly significant. She handed me an envelope, sealed, with these words. I made a note immediately after she left so that I should not forget the exact phrasing."

The lawyer rummaged in his papers while Bray sat back with the joyful feeling of a hound joining in a full cry on a perfect scent. Tarr handed a slip of paper over to Bray. On it was written:

"If any suspicious circumstances should surround Mrs Budge's death, she would like this envelope to be handed to the police. If I were perfectly satisfied the death was natural, it is to be destroyed without being opened."

Mr Tarr handed the sealed envelope to the detective. "I suggest that as her legal adviser it should be opened in my presence," he said, in a professional voice from which he was unable to eliminate all traces of curiosity.

Bray opened the envelope and read it. There was a long silence.

The lawyer fingered the wings of his collar.

Bray looked up and said gravely: "This is pretty nearly a death warrant."

Tarr literally grabbed the document. The last communication of Mrs Budge was brief and to the point.

"The will that I have made this day in favour of George Edward Budge was made as a result of threats of violence from him, and not of my own free will. He is not my husband in the eyes of the law, and I hereby declare that any bequest in his favour was made wholly under duress.

"LOUISA DEERING,

"(known as LOUISA BUDGE)."

Chapter Nine

BUDGE VERSUS BRAY: FIRST ROUND

"What about that chat we were going to have?" Charles asked Bray. "And are there going to be any developments to give me a really good story to-day?"

Bray had met Charles on his return to the hotel from the lawyer's.

"To be perfectly candid," answered Bray, "and this is not for publication, I shall probably make an arrest to-day."

Charles looked astonished. "Quick work," he acknowledged. "Poor old Budge!"

A police detective should be immune to minor human failings, but Bray was distinctly irritated by the fact that Charles had reached a right conclusion so effortlessly, even if he had jumped to it.

"Yes, as a matter of fact it is Budge," he admitted. "Was it a guess?"

"Mainly guess-work," acknowledged Charles. "Budge was the obvious murderer from the point of view of opportunity. Of course, he did not do it. Can you imagine a laundry proprietor neatly dismembering a body, when he has only got to put it in one of his machines to tear it to unrecognizable pieces, judging by the condition in which my shirts return from the wash?"

Bray laughed. "I really believe those are the sort of grounds on which you would condemn or acquit a man, Charles," he said, with a hint of patronage. "Unfortunately we have to work on more commonplace lines at the Yard. Budge not only had the opportunity, he had the motive, and even if we have to tear the hotel to bits we'll find evidence to prove he did the dismemberment."

Charles leaned back and regarded Bray severely through his eyeglass. "I believe you are suspecting poor old Budge simply because you have at last found he threatened to murder his wife if she did not make a will in his favour."

For a moment Bray goggled. He looked at Charles with a face eloquent of suspicion. "How the devil did you find that out?" he asked.

"Elementary, my dear Watson," he said. "I deduced it as exactly the type of motive which would make the Yard believe Budge was the murderer."

"Bah!" growled Bray. "How did you find out?"

Charles relented and told him of the conversation he had overheard on his first visit to the Garden Hotel.

"There you are," said the detective triumphantly. "You'll have to tell that in the witness-box before you are much older."

"Well, I don't believe our poor old lay reader did it for one moment," Charles said. "And if you can spare the time, I would like to unfold a theory of my own as to a certain gentleman who could tell you a good deal more than he has done about this affair."

"Sorry, I can't spare any time—for your theories," retorted Bray rudely. "I'm going to have a little talk with Budge. But for old times' sake, and on condition you make no use of what you hear without my permission and because you're going to be a witness for the prosecution, you can come with me when I interview Budge."

"All right," said Charles, "but it amazes me to see still, after all the detective novels that have been written, how little Scotland Yard heeds the amateur whose brilliant deductions are so inevitably right." And Charles followed with exaggerated dejection in Bray's wake.

On the way Bray met Billings, who drew Bray aside. "Come and look at the laundry basket in Budge's room," he said.

Bray's eyes brightened with interest.

Billings opened the basket with the air of a conjurer, and Charles was disappointed to find it empty. The two policeman bent over it eagerly while Billings pointed out in turn the places from which had been taken a human hair and a couple of strands of white thread which now were enclosed in marked transparent envelopes.

"The hair is identical in texture and colour with Mrs Budge's," he said, his big fingers, surprisingly deft, emphasizing his points. "The threads match the fabric of her nightdress, and I have, I think, found the place from which they were torn. On the face of it, it seems certain that the body was thrust into this basket for a time. It must have been a tight fit, and there are certain deformations—here, for instance, and here—which support the theory."

Bray smiled irritatingly at Charles. "Better and better," he said. His face clouded for a moment. "If the body was placed in here immediately, it seems almost incredible that Noakes should have overlooked it when he searched the room immediately afterwards."

"Once he had it in the basket," said Charles helpfully, "he could move it about fairly quickly. Probably hid it in another room while the Sergeant was searching this room, and then moved it back when there was an opportunity or when the other room was due to be searched—a grim sort of version of a nursery game called *hunt the slipper*."

Bray thought for a moment, thinking back along the time-table so industriously prepared by Noakes. "Yes, that's possible," he conceded, "and it would enable him in a large measure to choose the time and place for the dismemberment of the body. Have you discovered anything else, Billings?" he added.

"Not yet, Inspector," the man replied. "But it is a fairly slow business in a show as big as this hotel."

"Well, carry on then and report progress."

Billings saluted and went.

"It's been my experience," remarked Bray, "that when one has once started to get one's line on the culprit things start to happen, and you know by the way clues multiply one is on the right trail. If we could only get a line on the dismemberment connecting it with Budge, I should have the case in my pocket."

"Come, come, you're losing faith," said Charles. "Square your shoulders, remember your duty, forget the Judges' rules, and pile into Budge."

I I

"I suppose I am the only resident in the Garden Hotel who hasn't a theory about the murderer," complained Miss Sanctuary to Viola. "Nearly everyone has come up to me at one time or other and unfolded their pet hypothesis with the hope of getting me to support them." She sighed. "And all I can do is to say that I can't help them at all, that I can only remember one little unimportant thing and I have already told that to the police."

Miss Sanctuary was sitting in the little room on the ground floor which, although a common room, had been accepted as her special retreat. Viola's imagination boggled at the square yardage of knitting which had been turned out in the room since her arrival. The steady click of Miss Sanctuary's needles—or was it the kind face with the piercing eyes—must have had some restful quality, for Viola was not the first to drift into that room and talk with its grey-haired occupant. Viola felt herself a little closer to sanity now that she had done so. She had rushed out of the lounge, in the middle of a heated discussion on the Coptic rite between Blood and Eppoliki, with a strong desire to scream. She felt better now.

"The most disappointing part of the whole affair," she said, "is that the five people who are all likely candidates for the position of murderer have such perfect alibis. Eppoliki, for instance, the sinister Oriental with a past, Mrs Walton, so unexpected a murderer that the wary detective would be bound to suspect her; and, of course, Charles and myself, even more suspicious, perhaps, than Mrs Walton."

"I'm glad you read detective stories, my dear," commented Miss Sanctuary. "So do I. And I should say that even your alibi isn't perfect. We can't prove that the murder was done at the time of your bridge game, or that the person who assaulted me was the murderer. You know at one time I had the fantastic idea that it was Mrs Budge herself who attacked me."

"What a priceless idea!" exclaimed Viola. "I really believe that you would make a splendid detective if you would only try. Think of the advantage of sitting here and having everyone come and tell you their secrets."

Miss Sanctuary smiled. "Perhaps I shall offer to help the police if they appear to be stuck. Meanwhile I'll give you a little information. I think the police are going to arrest poor Mr Budge. I happen to know that things look rather black against him, and there was a blood-thirsty gleam in Inspector Bray's eye when he looked in here just now."

"Well, I'm sure they're wrong," declared Viola. "Poor little man! I hope he gets off."

"Scotland Yard never makes a mistake," asserted Miss Sanctuary positively; but perhaps there was a twinkle in her eye.

III

The two walked into the now famous sitting-room (Charles's minute description in the *Mercury* was familiar to every *Mercury* reader) in the Budges' suite. Budge was sitting at a table going through a pile of correspondence and gazing with disapproval at the two burly members of the Force who were crawling about the bedroom floor and taking numberless and apparently pointless measurements of the distance of this article from that and their respective heights.

"Sorry if I haven't been very helpful, Inspector," said the unwitting quarry of the law, leaning back in his swivel chair. "Everything has been at sixes and sevens since this shocking affair, and I have had my hands full keeping the hotel going."

"Well, perhaps you can spare some of your time now," answered the Inspector coldly, planking down his chair in the window with so obvious a gesture that the other, unless he were extremely dense, could not fail to see that he was to be the object of close scrutiny during the conversation.

"Fire away," Budge said. His tone was noncommittal and his face expressionless, but Charles saw his Adam's apple bob twice above his collar, as patent a signal of distress as if he had licked his lips.

"Matters have come to the knowledge of the police, Mr Budge," began Bray portentously, "which refer to a time prior to the death of your wife. You will, no doubt, realize well enough that you need make no statement which will incriminate yourself, but I am going to ask you if you can throw light on this subject."

While Bray was speaking, with a careful choice of words, the colour slowly drained from the man's face, leaving it the colour of dry parchment. His little eyes darted round the room, and he paused for a full minute before he spoke.

When at last the words came, the voice was hoarse with fear but the tone was the tone of resignation. "I knew it would come out sooner or later," he said. "I'd best make a clean breast of it."

Here Bray made an error, pardonable enough in the circumstances, but one for which he kicked himself a thousand times in after days. "Never prompt a confession" was a rule in which, as a keen amateur psychologist, he had a profound belief. But now he broke it.

"You had better do so," he said. "The police have evidence of your threat to your wife from two different sources."

Budge's face was a study. For a moment it was a battleground of the emotions. The colour ebbed back to his face and his expression of fear changed to one of surprise.

"You mean——" he asked, and stopped.

"I mean," retorted Bray, as irritated as a hunter who feels his quarry eluding his grasp with a wriggle of unexpected strength, "that your wife's lawyer handed me this," and he passed the document to Budge.

Budge read it once. He read it again, slowly, and Charles perceived that he was thinking quickly and desperately while he stared at the fatal message from the woman who had been called Mrs Budge.

"My God!" he said at last. "The bitch!"

The Inspector looked at him sternly. "We have evidence confirming the fact that you threatened your wife," he said.

Budge's eyes were now like gimlets, and they fastened calmly, if warily, on the Inspector's. Gone was the furtiveness and fear of a few minutes ago. Charles felt the change in the temper of the interview, not without malicious satisfaction. It was as if during a duel one of the antagonists had tripped and bright death had quivered for a moment at his heart. Some miracle had enabled the threatened man to regain his feet, and now he was on level terms, fighting for his life with the chances at least not in his disfavour. Bray, to whom the change was equally obvious, gave no other sign of irritation than a mounting colour.

"My dear Inspector, it is obvious you are a bachelor," replied the other. "Otherwise you would be aware that in a married quarrel it is no rare thing for a husband to offer to wring his wife's neck. But you could hardly hold the position you do without some knowledge of human nature. Do you think any jury would convict on the evidence of a threat as between husband and wife? The woman was hysterical when she wrote this, and had it not been for this tragedy, she would have called on her solicitors in a day or two and got the note back. Where's the motive?"

Bray did not take offence at the calculated insolence of the other's tone. "The motive was an estate of, let me say, something over £100,000."

The thrust told. Budge attempted no riposte.

"In addition, you were seen by Nurse Evans leaving the only possible exit from the room where the murder took place immediately after the probable time of the murder," went on Bray. "We have positive evidence that your wife's body was in your bedroom for a period," he added quietly.

Budge rose and looked down at his interrogator. "I swear before God that I had no hand in the murder of my wife," he said earnestly. "Find who did that foul work with the body, and then perhaps you will be on the track of the man you want. I tell you here and now, Inspector, that there's more in this than meets the eye, and you won't be able to clap your handcuffs on the murderer as easily as you think. Do I look like an intelligent man, and do you think I would harm a hair of my wife's head as long as I was sharing in her income while she lived and was left it when she died a natural death? If you'd asked Tarr, Inspector, whether my wife, poor soul, ever grudged me any sum I liked to draw, you'd have been less ready to take notice of the hysterical doings of an overwrought woman."

Bray rose also to his feet. "I don't propose to beat about the bush any longer," he said. "Let us assume you are as innocent as you state. So far I have not accused you, nor shall I do so until I have given you the statutory caution and have the warrant in my pocket. But you know a great deal that has a bearing on the case and you have not been frank with me. If you are innocent, any help in the solution of this mystery that you can give will help in establishing that innocence. Not to give it renders you liable to a charge as accessory."

"You've already as good as accused me of the murder," the man retorted sullenly. "I'm damned if I say a word."

The suave outlines of Bray's face sharpened with temper. "Well, you'll cool your heels in prison for a little."

"You can't do that without a warrant," Budge retorted instantly.

"Oh, yes, we can," replied the other. "We will detain you as an important witness."

Charles waited with amusement to see how Bray's bluff would work. Its effect was unexpected. Budge laughed loudly with the forced tone of one who laughs seldom.

"So you'd put me in prison, would you?" he said at last. "Well, all I can say is this—do that, and by God you'll see hell let loose in this hotel, clever Mr Policeman."

Bray, skilled to detect the undercurrents of a witness's emotions, realized that Budge was in earnest. The thought of prison had scared him less than the prospect of what would happen if he were away from the Garden Hotel. For a moment he was perturbed.

Meanwhile Budge stood, his brow wrinkled with thought. "Look here, Inspector," he said after a time. "I've told you there's more in this than meets the eye. Will you give me half an hour to myself if I guarantee to bring at the end of that period positive proof that I had nothing to do with this business?"

Bray hesitated. His case was incomplete and he could not possibly risk detaining on suspicion at this stage.

"Right," he said. "I'll stay here, but you mustn't leave the building."

"Thank you," Budge answered, and left the room.

Bray called in Billings. "See that Budge does not leave this hotel," he said. "He can do what he likes otherwise. Don't trail him—just keep an eye on the exits."

IV

"Now, 'fountain of all knowledge,' tell us how, in your opinion, Budge managed to commit this murder?" asked Charles.

"The reconstruction is fairly easy," answered Bray. "The only point is how did Budge originally get in the room? He may have slipped in through the window after waiting outside on the verandah until Miss Sanctuary's back was turned. Alternatively he was already concealed in the room; the wardrobe would have made an excellent hiding-place, as quite a good view can be obtained from inside if one puts one's eye to the crack in the door."

"How thorough of you!" exclaimed Charles in admiration. "I never thought of crawling into the wardrobe. What fun you detectives have!"

"So far, so good," Bray continued imperturbably. "When Miss Sanctuary went to the door and was absorbed in conversation, he crept up, put out the light, which is near the door, and grabbed her from behind. As you will have noticed, the bedroom door has one of those tricky locks which, even with the key in them, will lock automatically if slammed. As he dragged her back, therefore, he could slam the door with his foot and she would be at his mercy, unable to recognize him. He knocked her unconscious, and then put on the light and tied her up. He thought she would be unable to identify him. Actually she does remember something. Her assailant wore a ring with an ornamental band on his left hand." Bray paused impressively. "So has Budge."

"That is interesting," Charles answered slowly. He seemed immersed in thought. "Dash it all though, thousands of people must wear rings like that—it might so easily be a coincidence."

"It might," agreed Bray. "Taken by itself it means nothing. In conjunction with the motive and the means and the basket in Budge's room, however, it takes the place of the material clue. It is a link in the chain.

"Budge then, in my opinion, disposed of Miss Sanctuary in the wardrobe so that if she came to, she would not be able to identify him. This was shrewd. Blindfolding would not be certain enough to make sure that she did not have some clue to his identity. When she was locked in the wardrobe, his mind would be at ease.

"He now turned his attention to his unconscious wife. He garrotted her quickly and neatly, and hauled her body out of bed, bundled it into the next verandah, and stuffed it into a laundry basket before the onset of *rigor mortis*.

"He would excite no suspicion or comment dragging about his precious laundry baskets. As you helpfully suggested, it would be very easy to stow it in a room until the police had searched the suite, and then put it back again, to dispose of it at his leisure."

"A method of disposal," pointed out Charles, "which, according to your own man, Wuthering, needed the skill of at least a G.P. or a medical student."

"He may have had some such experience," said Bray. "So far I have been able to discover absolutely nothing about the life of either before they came to the hotel."

Charles shook his head slowly. "That's an ingenious reconstruction, but it does not point to Budge more than anyone else. Your case isn't complete, and you know it in your heart of hearts."

"Wait and see," answered Bray grimly.

"Aren't you afraid that now he is cornered he may take poison or jump out of the window?" asked Charles ingenuously.

"Murderers never commit suicide except in novels," answered his friend abstractedly. "The two types are poles apart." Looking up suddenly he met Charles's grin and realized that his leg was being pulled. He smiled in acknowledgment. "Do you really think that Budge is going to return with any proof of his innocence that we can't riddle with holes?"

"I not only think but know," answered Charles complacently.

Jamming in his eyeglass, he picked up a copy of the *Mercury* which lay on the table and re-read his story for the third time, while the clock ticked out the seconds and Bray went into the bedroom and looked at the results of his men's labours in plans and potential clues. They were disappointing, and he returned twenty-five minutes later to find Charles looking at his relinquished society gossip column with an expression of acute distaste. His deputy was not wasting his chances. Six paragraphs were devoted to a description of the decoration of the new flat of his inamorata.

"Pink bathrooms!" exclaimed Charles in disgust.

There was a knock on the door and Budge came silently in, followed by the gaunt figure of Miss Mumby and the bald corpulence of Winterton. They stood sheepishly beside Budge.

"I saw both these people on the night of the murder," he said, without preamble. "I think they can satisfy you that your suspicions are unfounded."

Bray raised an inquiring eyebrow at Miss Mumby.

"On the night of the murder," said Miss Mumby at once, staring Bray in the eyes, "Mr Budge came to my suite to discuss some damage which he said my pets had done in the lounge. We discussed it for about half an hour, and he left at a minute or two before nine-thirty."

"You are as certain of the time as that?" asked Bray incredulously.

"Certainly. Before he left he remarked that my clock was ten minutes slow and that it was really nine-twenty-eight. I put the clock on but still could not believe he was right until I heard St Michael's clock strike over the road, which proved he was right."

Bray turned to Winterton.

"Mr Budge called on me in my room on the night of the murder," Winterton affirmed, "with reference to a complaint I had made about some shirts I had sent to the laundry. The way the neckbands were stretched and the collars shrunk was really intolerable, and I wrote to Budge and told him so. I remember quite well that directly Budge came into the room he said he had had a slight argument with Miss Mumby about the time. We compared watches, and we both made it twenty-six minutes to ten. Budge did not stay long—just long enough to promise to look into the matter, apologized very handsomely I must say—I fancy it was about ten minutes."

Winterton clicked audibly and stared at the policeman defiantly.

Bray's sensations can only be compared to those of a man who steps on a stair that isn't there; or to those of a greyhound pursuing an electric hare round a track, when it suddenly vanishes. Budge's movements were now completely accounted for without a moment to spare. After speaking to Miss Mumby he had gone straight to his bedroom, looked in, and without waiting a second had gone on to Winterton's room. He could only just have left Winterton's room a minute when Nurse Evans had found him again on the point of leaving his bedroom.

Baulked of his hare, Bray still, like the greyhounds, persisted in sniffing for a little round the hole.

"Why did neither of you tell me this when I was investigating the movements of everyone in the hotel yesterday?" he asked sternly.

Winterton looked at him with a bovine stare. "I didn't see what my complaint about shirts had to do with the murder," he said stubbornly.

Bray made a last effort. "You will both be prepared to swear to every detail of this story in a court of law?" he pressed.

"Certainly," snapped Miss Mumby.

"Of course," puffed Winterton.

"Very well then," said the Inspector, bowing to the inevitable. "That accounts satisfactorily for your movements, Budge, and there the matter can rest for a moment."

"Thank you, Inspector," replied Budge cheerily. "I hope you will realize that you exceeded your duty a little."

His remark drew fire from the detective's grey-blue eyes, but he said nothing.

Budge turned and left. Miss Mumby, with gawky strides, followed in his rear. Winterton shuffled deprecatingly out after them, polishing his head with his handkerchief.

As the door closed, Charles spoke. "O, frabjous morn, Callooh, Callay," he chortled, whirling his monocle till it made a shining disc of fire. "What a perfectly incredibly marvellously watertight alibi."

For a moment Bray looked as if he would explode. Seizing a large pouffe as the only available safety-valve, he hurled it with all his force at the door.

"Yes, I can imagine how you feel," cooed Charles sympathetically.

Chapter Ten

MISS MUMBY GIVES THE SHOW AWAY

"Of course, this sort of thing is always happening," Bray said with philosophic resignation when he met Charles an hour later. "One generally bangs one's head against three brick walls before one finds the right turning. In a sense the perfection of Budge's alibi is a help. It definitely excludes him from my list of suspects, and I have to go right back to the beginning and start again."

Charles could not but admire the infinite patience of Scotland Yard in the genuine enthusiasm with which Bray cleaned his slate of hypotheses and started again.

"The devil of this case is that as it is an inside job," went on Bray gloomily, "there is not likely to be any clue connecting the murderer obviously with his victim. Each of my suspects, for instance, have probably been in Mrs Budge's suite heaps of times, and might have left foot-prints all over the ceiling for all the use it would be."

"Do not despair," Charles answered comfortingly. "Remember motive, the policeman's friend."

"Yes," answered Bray. "This case is going to be solved on the question of motive, if at all. There are some strange features about this ordinary-looking hotel, and if we can get to the bottom of them we may run our motive to earth at the same time."

"What do you think particularly curious?" asked Charles.

Bray told him briefly of Mrs Budge's inexplicably large income. "That's not all," Bray went on. "Hasn't it occurred to you as strange that in this hotel, with the proprietress murdered and policemen perpetually clumping over the place, no one has attempted to leave?"

"Presumably you have refused to let them?"

Bray snorted. "The police can't do that sort of thing in real life. As long as they kept in touch with us they are perfectly free to move—and yet they don't." He shook his head, puzzled.

"So far as I can see from the business records, the hotel has always been run in a perfectly straightforward manner. It was started five years ago, and the Rev. Septimus Blood, Mr Winterton and Miss Mumby moved in at once. A Samuel Eggfeldt was the next guest, and he stayed until he was run over and killed in a street accident. During the remainder of the time, Mr Nicholas Twing, Colonel Cantrip, the Misses Geranium and Hectoring, Eppoliki and Mrs Walton all moved in. Mrs Walton, by the way, was to leave next week, as apparently she is a widow and is engaged to marry St Clair Addington. I got the tip from the Chief to save her all the bother I could. Addington and the Chief are old friends. Then the latest arrivals were Miss Arrow, who left after three months, Miss Sanctuary, Lady Viola and yourself. The only peculiarity is that everyone who has arrived here has, with one exception, stayed, but after all this is a residential hotel and apparently a very comfortable one, so there is really nothing very suspicious in that."

"If you are really yearning for something suspicious to fasten on," said Charles, "I can gratify your base appetite. The morning after the murder I called in to see the Rev. Septimus Blood. While I was there, Budge called for the laundry basket. Innocent enough request you will say, but Blood refused to let him have it—nearly knocked him down. Now Blood is not only a bacteriologist, he is a Bachelor of Medicine with considerable clinical experience. Putting two and two together, and noting that the laundry basket is of a size excessively convenient for the reception of a corpse, I suggest for your consideration that the body was in the basket at the time; and that Blood subsequently cut it up and distributed it in that charming way which has so appealed to us all. One might look uneasy with a skeleton in the cupboard, but that was nothing to Blood's uneasiness. I suggest the solution is the body in the basket."

For the second time that day Bray stared at Charles in amazement, this time amazement tinged with fury. "Why didn't you tell me this earlier?" he asked coldly.

"I tried to," Charles pointed out with sweet reasonableness, "but you would not give me a chance."

Bray's reply was unprintable. "I'm going to see the Rev. Septimus Blood anyway," he added, when he felt better. This time Charles did not accompany him...

I I

"How goes it, Charles?" asked Viola, leaning over his shoulder and looking at a pad on which Charles had written, after earnest thought for ten minutes, the following words:

"Up to a late hour there were no further developments in the Dismembered Body Mystery. Inspector Bray, however..."

"Rottenly," replied Charles, hurling the pad from him. "An hour ago the police were going to arrest Budge, and he turned up with a water-tight alibi. Now they think they are going to arrest Blood, but I feel quite certain that he is not guilty and will be able to prove it. Meanwhile nothing is happening and my reputation at the *Mercury* is dwindling."

"Poor boy," commiserated Viola, smiling. "What do you intend to do about it?"

"Do you know, it has suddenly occurred to me that I might find the murderer myself," said Charles, who had, in fact, been cherishing the idea ever since his interview with the Chief.

Viola laughed. "If you did, I should begin to suspect you of having brains. Have you decided on the culprit already?"

"No, but I've got a shadow of a suspicion," replied Charles, drawing a comic face on the pad, "a shred of an inkling," he added, surmounting it with a top hat, "of how the murder *might* have been done. Bray, of course, would laugh at it," he said bitterly, giving the face a beard, "but I've a good mind to follow it up."

"I shouldn't," remarked Viola unencouragingly. "I have a feeling if you follow up your intuitions you will make a priceless ass of yourself. Leave that to the professional."

"I suppose I am a professional," remarked Charles casually, jamming his eyeglass home and looking at her sternly. "I was a detective for two years."

"Are you really serious?"

He nodded solemnly. "Yes. I cannot reveal where I was employed"—he looked round in the manner of the stage conspirator—"but I have a genuine letter of thanks with deep regrets at my resignation from the organization that employed my services."

Viola looked at Charles closely, removed his eyeglass and brushed his hair down over his forehead. "Good heavens!" she exclaimed in awestruck tones. "I believe I have misjudged you. You are not such a fool as you try to look. Did you track down erring wives, or did you specialize in following husbands in Paris? ... But, after all," she added despairingly, "no detective could possibly play bridge as badly as you."

"Bridge isn't everything, my girl," answered Charles. "I'll show you something in a day or two, and then you'll be sorry you said 'No' that afternoon in the Dutch garden at Tankards."

"Dear old days," exclaimed Viola, quite suddenly and irritatingly finding her eyes go misty. "A few years in London makes me feel quite sentimental when I think of spring in the country with the lambs and the violets and the incredible quantities of mud. It was excruciatingly boring but really rather nice. Are you still as much in love with me?"

"Curiously enough I am," he said.

Viola looked at him. She patted his hand. "I am sorry, Charles, I shouldn't have said that, should I? You've been awfully nice, and really I'm beginning to feel rather tired of London. I suppose it is a sign of a hidden strain of domesticity asserting itself. If I'm not careful I shall find myself saying yes." She smiled at Charles.

"'Maybe I shan't ask you, Madam,' he said," retorted Charles haughtily, replacing his eyeglass. "What the devil has Bray been doing with Blood?"

III

The detective, on entering Blood's room somewhat perfunctorily, had been astonished to see an enormous cone of brilliantly embroidered fabric standing upright in the room. The cone was truncated, and surmounted by the dark little Gaelic head of Blood, blue jowled and rubicund, squinting at his reflection in the mirror.

"Oh, Lord," groaned the detective to himself, "another lunatic!"

Blood swept towards him. "Sit down, Inspector," he said cordially. "I suppose you don't happen to know anything about the Coptic rite?"

"I don't," answered the Inspector.

"I can't remember whether or no one wears a maniple with this cope," the parson complained.

The Inspector, who had been nurtured on Evangelical principles, looked somewhat shocked. "Millinery," he murmured to himself. More politely he said, "Do you know anything about dissection, Mr Blood?"

The parson glanced at him warily, and busied himself with the chains of his cope. Freeing himself, at length he spoke in an expressionless voice.

"I have a medical degree, but my province, of course, is bacteriology. Why?"

"Mrs Budge's corpse was dissected by an expert."

"Well?"

(Probably not so daft as he looks, thought Bray.)

"Do you think a man of, say, Eppoliki's experience capable of doing the job?"

"Don't trifle with me, Inspector," said Blood waspishly. "You didn't come here to ask me a question which could have been better answered by your experts. Do you suggest I had any hand in this ghastly business?"

"That is a question you could best answer yourself, sir," answered the Inspector. "You will realize that it is necessary for us to consider every possible hypothesis, and it is at least practicable for someone to have stowed the body temporarily in this room and dissected it on this table." He pointed to the glazed table about seven feet long, on which were a rack of test tubes containing cultures, a pipette and a few trays of gelatine. "The body might have been stowed anywhere—this basket would have made a good hiding-place, for instance."

He lifted the lid and scrutinized the inside with an acute glance.

Blood smiled mirthlessly. "Make a microscopic examination of it," he suggested.

Bray, sensitive enough to shades, felt that wherever the corpse had been disposed, Blood had no fears of its leaving traces in this basket. Anyway, he wasn't getting very much change out of the Welsh parson. He decided to make a personal appeal. Blood was humming to himself and folding up the cope.

"Very well, sir," he said, "I will lay all my cards on the table."

"Good. Let's see them."

"Information from a trustworthy source has been laid"— the Inspector secretly smiled at this description of Charles's wild guess—"that prior to the time of its dissection the body was, to your knowledge, in this room."

Blood flushed to the roots of his hair. "The swine," he said passionately. "There's a limit beyond which I won't be driven. Can't you see a yard, Inspector? The man who gave you that information could give it to you because he put the body there himself. Budge is the murderer, and he's in it up to his neck. He's pushed his impositions on me too far, though." The little man's face was an alarming study in swift chromatic changes. "To think that Budge had the colossal impertinence to accuse me to you when a few words from me would end the whole farce of this precious Garden Hotel!" His tone rose to a scream and his hands were flung outwards. "End it," he repeated decisively.

For the second time that day—and the last time in the course of his career—the detective intervened with a remark on the brink of a confession.

"To be perfectly fair," he answered, "the accusation did not come from Budge."

The parson looked puzzled, then comprehension dawned in his eyes. "Oh, it's that lanky fellow, Venables, is it? He's not such an ass as he looks! I suppose I gave myself away pretty completely. Well, I'm glad Budge had the sense not to push his little joke too far."

The Inspector waited, but Blood said no more.

"You were saying," he prompted.

The parson looked at him sullenly. "I forget. In any case your information is pure inference and utterly without foundation. I defy you to prove that I knew anything about this affair, and I consider you are grossly exceeding your rights in badgering me in this manner. Did anyone see the body in my room? Did anyone see me dispose of it? The whole suggestion is monstrous and is a mere hypothesis founded on the fact that I have a doctor's degree."

"I am the best judge of that," said the Inspector sternly, changing his tone as he realized that Blood had said all he was likely to say. "I assume that as you have so little on your conscience you will have no objection to my having this room searched?"

Satisfied with this Parthian arrow, he went.

I V

Mrs Walton faced her tormentor. Budge, his face pursed up into a dry watchfulness, looked at her with the vacant, emotionless eyes of a reptile.

"You know more than you pretend," he snarled. "I believe you're in on this business! If I find out that you are connected with it in the remotest way, by God I'll end your little romance!"

Dry-eyed, Mrs Walton pressed her handkerchief wearily to her lips. "Why can't you let me alone? Haven't I paid for your silence—aren't I paying now?"

"Oh, yes, you're paying all right, and you'll go on paying. You'll be able to afford to pay a little more heavily in a month or two." He smiled wickedly.

"Oh, I'll pay, I'll pay," she said tonelessly. "What is the money compared to the hell of deception in which I live?" She rose and looked out of the window. "Sometimes I think I must end it all, make a clean breast of it whatever it costs. But I can't. I'm a coward, I suppose. It is like coming up against a blank wall suddenly. There it is, and it hardly seems a part of oneself, it's so permanent a barrier."

"Well, we must all pay for our little weaknesses. That's how I live, and so do a good many more, from doctors to judges." He turned on her suddenly. "Do you know who killed my wife?"

She looked at him, eyes steady. "No. If I did, I would thank him."

His eyes snapped fire. "Oh, you would, would you?" He addressed vacancy. "She'd thank him, she would," he mimicked, parodying her flash of spirit. "Well, my lady, I've more than a suspicion that you do know him, or if you don't, you have a pretty shrewd idea." He rose to his feet menacingly. "Now I'm not going to be caught so easily." He slapped his hip pocket. "I've got a little toy in there, and I know how to use it—I shan't hesitate to shoot, and I shall shoot to kill. What's more, if ever my suspicion proves a certainty, a certain document is going to Mr St Clair Addington by registered post, from an anonymous friend, with a little explanatory note. So tell that to your friend when you are thanking him."

His eyes bored into her, but she met them bravely. "You are mistaken," she answered, twisting her handkerchief. "Your wife and yourself must have made more than one enemy. You'd better look for danger from somebody who has refused to pay!"

V

"I'm quite sure that Blood is in it as deep as hell," concluded Bray, as he recounted the story of his fruitless interview, "but what is the good of knowing that if I can't lay my hands on some tangible clue or motive."

"Blood obviously knows a lot about it," said Charles. "Stubborn swine. It ought to be possible to make him own up, and one thing I'll swear. The sight of that corpse was a sheer surprise. He turned absolutely green."

"Anyway, I've given him a stiff warning and told him that we shall search his room," Bray answered.

"You never found the shawl Mrs Budge was wearing, did you?" said Charles thoughtfully.

"No, nor any instruments which could have been used for the dissection."

"How long ago did you leave Blood?"

"I came straight here—about ten minutes ago. Why?"

Charles disregarded the question. "Is there a fire in his room?"

"No, central heating. Why?" replied the astonished detective.

"He's not been out of the hotel to-day, has he?"

Bray looked puzzled. "What's your drift? I don't see it. He's not left the hotel to-day."

"Good," replied Charles. "I'm in possession of incriminating evidence. I have been interrupted trying to get rid of it. I can't burn it. I haven't been outside the hotel. Policemen in great boots are tramping up and down my corridor and I must get rid of it quickly—what do I do? Answer, follow me."

A look of comprehension relieved the surprise of the detective's face, and he followed Charles without demur. "Sound reasoning," he said. "I am much afraid, Charles, that you are going to turn into one of those brilliant amateur investigators who know who the murderer is from the start but have to let the fool from Scotland Yard blunder through eighteen chapters before they let the reader into their confidence."

Darkness was falling as they made their way into the yard at the bottom of the back wall of the main block of the hotel building. Black against the greying winter skies they could see the outlines of the two balconies of the Budge suite. Had they been standing in that place forty-eight hours or so earlier, they might have seen the ominous silhouette of Mrs Budge's assailant going and returning on his deadly work. Stare as they might now, the incident had drifted out of sight down the stream of time. Cunning, patience and perseverance might weave a fabric of circumstantial evidence which would satisfy the clear eyes of justice, but the sharp outlines of the deed as it had been actually done must inevitably remain for ever blurred by the mists of conjecture.

They stared up at the grey mass of the building. Blood's window was in darkness but the window itself was open.

They watched for ten minutes and then the curtains moved. The two pressed themselves into the shadow of the fire-escape. The dim outline of a head appeared at the window, peered downwards into the yard as if to pierce the blackest shadows, and then disappeared. Like the Lady of the Lake, a hand appeared, grasping a long baton-like object, and then Excalibur fell with a plop on the ground. The arm vanished again and the head took its place. It was apparently satisfied with its second scrutiny, for it appeared no more.

Bray walked quietly into the yard, grabbed his prize, and came back.

"All according to schedule," he said. "Come along."

In Charles's sitting-room they unwrapped Excalibur. His outward integument was composed of the shawl, of texture almost as Victorian as the furnishing of her bedroom, in which Mrs Budge had been dressed, according to the nurse's description. Rolled up neatly inside it were a set of dissecting scalpels and a saw, which Bray realized with resignation might have been bought second-hand at any shop for medical supplies.

"Blood may or may not be guilty," said Bray, "but I've a good mind to arrest him as an accessory and see if he'll speak."

VI

> "Speak, kindly voice, from out th' encircling gloom;
> Tell us life is, even beyond the tomb.
> Beyond the darkness lies our sunlit home;
> Speak, kindly voice, from out th' encircling gloom."

With the final "gloom," the door of the lounge opened and there was a patter of feline feet. The spiritualistic version of a popular hymn which was being sung by Miss Mumby was mournful at the best of times, but now her voice seemed to be staggering under a dead weight of dejection.

Charles was lounging in a deep chair with its back to the door. Miss Mumby's glance did not take him in—at any rate she continued singing with the self-confident air of the songster of indifferent voice who believes that he is unheard:

> "The darkness falls, and we are sore perplexed,
> With sceptic doubt and legal rigour vexed.
> Speak to us, voice, and cheer our workers on,
> Ye, too, were workers, in times past and gone."

Moved to his catty core, little Walter mewed plaintively. Charles stole a look at Miss Mumby. She was sitting in a chair and large teardrops were oozing from her eyes and coursing clammily down her cheeks.

A thought that had been loitering idly at the back of his mind suddenly sprang to attention. He checked his impulse to reveal his presence by a discreet cough or, discreeter still, a sudden snore. He watched her intently. She seemed absorbed in her thoughts. Presently, perhaps she would make the revealing movement for which he was waiting.

After five minutes it came. There was a quick mechanical glance right and left, which missed her watcher. Then Miss Mumby slowly opened her bag...

"My sainted aunt," murmured Charles to himself. "Oh, you idiot, you fool, you blind, deaf, crass blunder-head of a disgraced and defeated detective!" He wrestled with an inclination to kick himself violently and subdued it. "Three days and more to find out what was happening under my very nose!"

"Come on, Walter! Get up, Socrates!" commanded Miss Mumby clearly. Having, all unconsciously, advanced the mystery of the Garden Hotel on the road to solution, she rose and left the room. The door closed, but her voice, now raised militantly and enthusiastically, floated back to the lounge.

> "Onward, gifted mediums,
>   Onward to the fray!
> Spirit hands are round you
>   From the break of day.
>
> Hear the spirit voices
>   From the sunny land.
> Help them, gifted mediums!
>   Lend your helping hand!"

VII

"Well, there it is!" said Bray to his superior bitterly. "There are enough suspicious characters there to stock Dartmoor, yet I'm damned if I can lay a finger on one of them. They simply dance round me making long noses."

"I realize how hampered you are nowadays," said the Commissioner in an understanding tone that was not without its sting, "but the very fact that these people are so involved should place you in a position sufficiently strong to enable you to force some information out of them."

"The more information I get, the less the business makes sense," replied Bray. "Look at Blood—a perfect sitter for the murderer. No motive, of course, but"—he laughed sardonically—"we can't expect everything in this case. But the very evidence that put us on the track—Venables's story—also goes to show that he cannot have been the murderer, because the appearance of the corpse came as a complete surprise to him. Equally, of course, if he wasn't the murderer, why did he dispose of the body?"

"Perhaps he did the murder," suggested the Commissioner, "and then got rid of the body somewhere—perhaps planted it on Budge. Budge, we will say, returns the gift with thanks. Tableau—Blood's horror when he finds the body's back again and he's got to find some other means of disposing of it."

"Yes, sir, that hangs together," admitted Bray grudgingly. "It's rather like hunt the slipper," he said, unconsciously borrowing Charles's simile, "and the policeman is the mug while the residents of the Garden Hotel pass the body to each other behind their backs. If only they played according to the rules and we could hang the fellow who was caught with it."

"Cheer up," said the Commissioner, "you may do so yet." He looked at Bray keenly. "You have an excellent record. I regard this case as more important, however, than any that you have handled before. You understand?"

Bray understood perfectly.

Chapter Eleven

BUDGE VERSUS BRAY: SECOND ROUND

"Mrs Budge was in no way an hysterical woman," said her solicitor to Bray, surprised to hear that his client's dramatic document had proved useless. "In my considered opinion she wrote that letter in very real fear of her life. It is strange that her fear should have been so rapidly justified, and yet her ante-mortem accusation should prove false."

"It is curious," replied Bray, "but you will realize that Budge's alibi is absolutely unassailable in a court of law. The bill would be thrown out by the Grand Jury. I've put that line of investigation behind me and I am concentrating on motive now. I hope to get something useful out of tracing Mrs Budge's income."

"I gathered, when I saw your man Samuels yesterday," remarked Tarr, "that he was well on the way to solving that particular mystery. He seemed intensely amused, but refused to tell me why."

"Another disappointment, I suppose," growled Bray. "In the light of what I have told you, can you suggest any lines that would be worth following?"

Tarr thought for a moment. "I have certain documents which my client gave me. She said they were not intrinsically valuable, but had an intense sentimental interest, and would I look after them for her. I will get you the documents in question."

While the deed-box was being searched for, Tarr dropped for a moment his pose of a successful company promoter and became a little more the professional man.

"I'm rather distressed about this business," he confided. "My firm has never had—or wanted—a criminal practice, and while the good lady has done nothing illegal in being killed, one naturally feels a certain stigma when one of one's clients is murdered in such a very butcherly fashion."

Bray smiled. The attorney's distress was rather comical. "Most disturbing," he agreed.

The solicitor's explanation was cut short by the arrival of the deed-box. Tarr handed Bray two envelopes each marked "confidential" and heavily sealed, but contained in cheap manilla envelopes: one was blue-pencilled with an X and the other with a Y.

The lawyer watched the detective open them with some distaste and an air of acute apprehension.

"X" contained a collection of cuttings from papers all bearing a date of some five years ago. Some of them were provincial papers, others were London dailies. Each cutting dealt with a series of frauds which had been committed by a young man. The frauds were all identical in character—the young man had invented a chemical preparation which removed spots from clothes. Practical demonstration of this cleanser convinced credulous people that here was a magnificent patent preparation which had only to be exploited to bring in a fortune to its lucky backer. Sums ranging from £500 to £5,000 were advanced to float the company, but directly the money was forthcoming the persuasive young genius vanished, and his victim found that the cleanser worked so magically by virtue of a powerful acid which, two days after its application, left a corroded hole where the original stain had been. Finally, one mug had complained to the police, and although the trickster was never caught, sufficient publicity was given to his subtle idea to prevent anyone else falling a victim to his ingenuity.

There was no writing of any sort with the cuttings, and no clue to the identity of any of the persons referred to.

In the other envelope was a copy of a marriage certificate. The marriage was between Giovanni Sarto (30) and Mary Church (18) at a registry office in Coventry. This also was for a date some five years ago, and Bray noted that neither party had any permanent address.

Tarr looked at the documents in some surprise. "What do you make of these?" he asked innocently.

Bray chuckled. "They have a strong smell of blackmail."

The lawyer's face was a study. If the smell had been brimstone he could not have handed the document back to Bray more gingerly.

"Cheer up," said the detective, laughing. "Your client is beyond the reach of legal proceedings. If I might make a suggestion, it is that you would be safer in sticking to our impoverished but still reasonably law-abiding gentry. Good-bye."

I I

"Who was married five years ago in a Coventry registry office? Who was guilty of a series of frauds five years ago?" Bray, posing these questions to himself for the umpteenth time, felt that if he could find the answer to them he would at last be at grips with that elusive motive. Meanwhile, he awaited the report of Samuels in his little room at Scotland Yard with real impatience.

Punctual to the minute Samuels appeared. He greeted Bray coolly. Unfastening his valise with exasperating slowness, he extracted and arranged a multitude of papers. Samuels never failed to irritate Bray. Tall, weedy, with a tiny moustache, white pasty face and a thin, cylindrical, out-jutting nose that looked as if it were made of putty, he seemed to cultivate an aloofness to mark him out as something more than merely a policeman. His black coat and vest and wing collar were definitely professional, and he adopted the attitude not of a staff man, but of an outside professional adviser.

Nothing irritated Bray more than to be fixed with Samuels's

cold, squinting eye and favoured with his slow, sly grin when he was explaining to him the progress of an investigation. The look and smile seemed to say, "Don't drag me into that side of it, please. I am an accountant, not a copper." Bray, in his turn, retaliated by treating him as a captain of industry would treat his auditor when the latter was a member of a respectable but smallish firm. Relations would have been difficult between them had not each party a secret recognition of the efficiency of the other in his own particular sphere.

"Mrs Budge's books were in excellent order," said Samuels. "I have traced through all the income and expenditure responsible for the very considerable profit she made over a period of years, and with the help of the banks concerned have been able to vouch each transaction satisfactorily. You will be surprised to hear that there were very few cash receipts—they were nearly all in the form of drafts and therefore very easily traceable."

"Well, where did the money emanate from?" asked Bray impatiently.

"Mrs Budge appears to have been an extremely good business woman," said Samuels. "At any rate, she appears to have made her little hotel show a profit of many thousands a year."

The detective looked as discomfited as he felt. "It is impossible," he commented. "You must be mistaken, Samuels."

The other grinned deprecatingly. "I can assure you there can be no mistake. The majority of her guests paid, by monthly cheque, about £2,000 a year for the privilege of staying at the Garden Hotel."

An extraordinary possibility took shape in Bray's mind. "Blackmail," he murmured, "it must be! Mass blackmail!"

For a moment he was flabbergasted by the ingenuity—the amazing audacity—of the woman whose death had awakened the forces of the law. "What a mind!" he exclaimed. "It looks as if this priceless character ran an hotel for the sole purpose of blackmail—the hush-money charges being included in the bill."

The ludicrous side of the situation appealed to him. Samuels did not seem amused.

"That's your theory, is it, Inspector? Well, that's not my worry luckily. Here is an extract of the relevant books—with a schedule of the payments making up the *Receipts from Guests* items in the profit and loss accounts. There is also a schedule of the amounts paid by each guest.

"I don't think there will be any further queries, but in case there are, I am keeping the books in my office until your investigation is completed"—he paused a moment and added—"or abandoned."

Bray's first feeling of triumph gradually evaporated as he thought over the amazing turn his investigation had taken. Blackmail was an excellent motive to unearth for a crime, but blackmail on this gargantuan scale only made confusion twice confounded. Instead of eliminating the possible suspects, it multiplied them. Half the residents in the hotel were potential suspects, and what was worse, the sinister conjuration of blackmail evoked the possibilities of perjury, false evidence, and faked alibis. He felt as if the edifice of fact which during the last few days he had erected at any rate as far as the first story was already crumbling, its foundations sapped.

He pulled himself together and went again over the material facts. He felt that the only thing that was established was (*a*) that Budge had the motive to commit the murder but had had a perfect alibi, (*b*) that Blood, if he were blackmailed, had the motive for the crime, and was almost certainly responsible for the disposal of the corpse.

It was true that Charles felt certain that Blood was genuinely astonished at finding the body in his room. But if the murderer really had been playing hunt the slipper with the corpse, it might well have been that Blood might have bestowed the unwelcome cadaver in Budge's room, and that Budge found it and very astutely returned it to his own. Blood would then have been unpleasantly surprised enough at finding that the responsibility had been again thrown on him and, faced with the situation, he would have chosen the dissection and dispersal of the remains as the speediest and most certain means of eliminating the danger. He would probably have returned the laundry basket to Budge's room with its evidence in the shape of a human hair and a shred of cloth and exchanged it for Budge's own innocent basket. This would account for his equanimity when Bray inspected the basket in his room.

This possibility, suggested by the Commissioner, had not struck Bray before as very attractive because then the essential motive was absent. Now, however, it was clear that Blood was paying a heavy yearly tribute to Mrs Budge as the price of silence. Bray, who knew a little of Blood's type, the enthusiastic revivalist who was still the ordinary sensual man with all the implacable drive and cunning fury of the Celt, could well imagine Blood choosing to end an arrangement which might eventually become intolerably irksome.

Bray had the feeling that comes to the inexperienced swimmer who has ventured out of his depth and after much exertion but little forward progress feels at last firm ground beneath his toes. As he revolved the situation in his mind and leaned back in his chair, he reached for his tobacco—sure sign to those who knew him that he was seeing light.

Bray, with his pipe going well, decided to tackle Blood again next day. First, however, he would ascertain how much hush-money Blood had paid over in the course of his stay in the clutches of the proprietress of the Garden Hotel. He routed out the schedule to which Samuels had referred and looked at it.

Mingled wonder, disgust and irritation were in the snort with which he put down his pipe and stared unbelievingly at the figures.

The schedule was divided into two tables. In the first were the people who were paying £2,000 a year for the privilege of a room in this little Kensington hotel. In the second were those who were paying a reasonable figure, varying from three guineas to six guineas a week according to the suite.

In the second division were Charles, Lady Viola, Miss Arrow, Miss Sanctuary *and the Rev. Septimus Blood!*

For the second time in the case Bray saw his carefully reared house of cards collapse. For the second time he faced defeat philosophically and turned back again to fundamentals.

He ran his eye down the people in Table A—all people who, if his theory was correct, had been ransoming their freedoms and their reputations to support one of the most ingenious blackmailing schemes ever devised.

The list was as follows:

Mr Nicholas Twing.
Miss Mumby.
Samuel Eggfeldt (deceased).
Mr Winterton.
Colonel Cantrip.
The Misses Geranium and Hectoring.
Mrs Walton.
Mrs Salterton-Deeley.

For a moment Bray was staggered at the implications of his theory. Admittedly, the guests at the Garden Hotel were a queer bunch with eccentricity sticking out all over them, but he felt it difficult to believe that one and all had pasts sufficiently murky to place them at the mercy of the parasite who battens on the rotten wood of society.

Yet what other conceivable alternative was there? And did it not seem that Budge had succeeded his wife in that revolting trade, and that still the guests of the Garden Hotel were immured in a moral prison, and paying richly for the privilege of their confinement? The repulsion which the blackmailer always roused in him filled

Bray's mind almost to the exclusion of his task of investigation, and he determined to put an end to that tyranny without delay.

Suddenly a thought struck him. If Budge had Miss Mumby and Winterton in his power, nothing would be easier than to concoct an alibi and force them to support it. Of course! The cool audacity with which Budge had walked out of the room when in danger of imminent arrest and invented an alibi while the detective and Charles kicked their heels and waited, filled him with unwilling admiration. It was of a piece with the whole grandiose scheme. The Budges, if his theories were correct, belonged to the first flight of criminal brain. Although he could probably put a term to the extortions from the hapless residents of the Garden Hotel, it might not be easy to get a conviction for blackmail. But if he could break down Budge's alibi, the blackmailer would be forced to face the capital charge, and his victims would be rid for ever of their tormentor.

The detective realized he would have to play his cards carefully. He had looked on the residents of the hotel hitherto as ordinary law-abiding citizens, ready to help the cause of justice so far as they could without inconveniencing themselves. Now, goodness knows what dark distrust of the law might be seething in their minds. He might look for double dealing everywhere, and could only be thankful that he was forewarned of the situation and could separate the sheep from the goats.

III

Charles accosted Bray with a start of exaggerated surprise.

"You're on the warpath, Bray," he exclaimed. "Who are you arresting to-day? Remember Punch's advice and don't."

Charles was full of spirits. The exclusive story of the finding of Mrs Budge's shawl and the scalpels had appeared in the *Mercury*, though naturally with no allusion to the way in which they were found. On the top of that he felt that he had in his hand a thread which, if he followed it aright, would conduct him to the centre of the maze. For the moment he preferred not to trust it to the clumsy tugging of the police, at any rate till he was a bit surer of where it was leading to.

Bray was preoccupied. He told briefly of his remarkable discovery. Charles, at first incredulous, was later delighted by the idea.

"Bray, I did not think you had it in you! You have the imagination of an Edgar Wallace. Fancy seven people all being peacefully and steadily blackmailed, as one of the extras in their *en pension* hotel bills."

Bray looked stubborn. "Can you suggest any other explanation?"

"Lots," said Charles. "This won't be the first hotel that's overcharged its guests. But after all—blackmail isn't a profession. It is easy for a blackmailer to get one victim; two is quite possible; three is improbable; four is impossible; seven is beyond the bounds of fantasy! Don't you see that the risks are immense! Sooner or later one of them is bound to squeak—or is it squeal? No seven people would stand a permanent arrangement of this kind. It is the whole strength of the blackmailer that his victim thinks each time is the last."

"You are not correct there, Charles," countered Bray. "I have had the status of these people investigated and they all could find the sum demanded without trouble, except possibly Mrs Walton, whose sources of income are rather mysterious. All the others would find no difficulty in the annual sum with which they purchased immunity."

"That's a good point," admitted Charles. "Still, it seems to me ridiculously unnecessary to make your victims reside in your own establishment." He paused. "Still, you are evidently unconvinced, so I will not favour you with my own poor suspicions."

"I should know fairly certainly in the next hour or so if my theory's right," was the detective's parting remark. "I'm going to see if I can smash that alibi of Budge's."

IV

Winterton was plainly not altogether surprised to see the detective. He sucked his teeth with a despairing sigh and offered him the hospitality of a deep leather armchair. The cordiality with which he plied him with drinks was insincere.

Bray had a delicate situation. He took his time. A little judicious silence did more to intimidate a witness than any amount of blustering.

Winterton reconnoitred Bray warily. He didn't quite know where to place him—the Force had changed a lot in his day. This fellow in his well-cut lounge suit with the plastered-back hair and the pale, clear-cut profile—in his, Winterton's time, if a fellow of that stamp had had any truck with the law, he would have been wearing the wig and gown of advocacy rather than the elegant mufti of the gentleman sleuth-hound.

Eventually speculation wore itself out, and Winterton found the silence oppressive. He broke it. "Well, Inspector," he said cheerily—he hoped, "what can I do for you?"

Bray hesitated. "Mr Winterton," he said, and he looked fixedly at his glass and not at the darting eyes of the other, "I should like to speak to you for a little as a legal adviser rather than as an officer of the law."

Bray's eyes were fixed on the swirling amber fluid, but he sensed the other tensing himself with suspicion.

"It happens repeatedly that a citizen by some indiscretion or slip in his past places himself in the power of another. If that other takes advantage of the situation to extort a valuable thing from his victim, then I cannot make it too clear that the law regards the affair with such abhorrence that there is almost no step it will not take, and no offence it will not condone, in order that the guilty shall be brought to book and his victim safeguarded."

Bray raised his eyes to Winterton's and he held them. They were like black lumps of toffee—completely expressionless.

"I cannot give you any official guarantees or assurances of indemnity, but speaking to you as man to man, I say to you that if you wish to reconsider the statement you made to me yesterday, no jot or tittle of harm can come to you, but that if you do not"—the detective's voice grew stern—"you will retard but not obstruct the progress of justice. The police can have no consideration for the member of society who wilfully persists as accessory after the fact in a capital charge."

The lumps of toffee swivelled and a pale tongue shot out and licked a pale mouth. Then Winterton broke out in high-pitched, metallic laughter.

"Really, Inspector, what a humorous situation. I believe you have a fixed conviction that I have been blackmailed into giving poor old Budge an alibi! God bless my soul, what incurable romanticists you detectives are! I had no idea Scotland Yard was so like the pictures!"

Bray felt as if he had been slapped in the face. His eyes snapped fire. "As you prefer. If we get Budge, as we probably shall in the end, we shall see you in the dock as accessory. If we don't, then you can go on paying him tribute for the rest of your life."

The detective slammed the door. Above the slam he heard the crackle of Winterton's high-pitched cackling.

Left to himself, Winterton was still amused. "Blackmail! That's a good one," he said to himself, and tottered to the sideboard.

V

Miss Mumby was not amused, she was annoyed. Bray approached the subject with such careful skirmishing that she professed to be unable to understand what he was driving at. When she did, her face was a mask of cunning fury. Bray had noticed that people grew like animals if they lived too much with them, and now Miss Mumby looked like a gaunt grey tabby, surly with age, spitting rage at a boy who had been tormenting her.

"I see," she hissed. (Bray realized for the first time that it was possible to hiss—the sibilance of her s's made the cat, which was lying on her lap, leap on to the floor.) "The law must have its victim and so I am to be accused of perjury, and not content with that, it is suggested that there are incidents in my past I am ashamed of." Her grey eyes glittered with scorn. "I'm a lonely woman now, and I suppose you policemen think you can ride rough-shod over me. I can tell you that if General Mumby had been alive he would have horse-whipped the man who made the suggestion you have made to me, policeman or no policeman. We may not be one of the great families of the world, but no one has ever said a word against the respectability of the Mumbys of Wick." She snorted indescribably, and her voice rose two octaves. "Let me tell you General Mumby knew Superintendent MacEwan of Scotland Yard, and if I tell him how the daughter of his friend has been treated, we'll see if he won't have your coat off your back."

"I think you must know there is more justification for my questions than you affect to believe, madam," replied the detective stiffly, when her invective had overflowed and subsided. "However, I withdraw any remarks I may have made in the course of my duty."

Bray did not stand upon the order of his going, but went.

"Dangerous old cat. I'm quite sure her annoyance was acted. What a hell of a case! Every time I think I'm on the right road I come up against a brick wall! I would give up all hope of promotion and pay for the opportunity of putting some of these people on the rack and getting the real truth out of them. I've never felt so sympathetic with the Inquisition. I suppose I must try Budge now."

VI

Budge was genially impertinent. "Really, Inspector, I have the fullest sympathy with your zeal, and am more anxious than you are to see my wife's murderer brought to book, but why it should help you to pry into our affairs, I don't know."

The detective was woodenly persistent. "Why do some of your guests pay £2,000 a year for staying in a small residential hotel in Kensington?"

The other adopted an attitude of engaging candour. "Ah, there you have me, Inspector. If we were as rich as Miss Mumby, for instance, it would be gay Paree for us." He winked familiarly. "But my wife was a far-seeing woman, and she realized that there were some rich people who wanted quietness and home comforts and would pay anything in reason for it."

The Inspector exploded. "And yet Mr Venables and Lady Viola and Miss Sanctuary and Miss Arrow and Mr Blood paid a tenth of the price for the same thing!"

"Ah, there you are," went on Budge shamelessly. "My wife realized that the poor things would be dull if there was no one else, so we took in a few charming souls at prices that didn't really pay us, in order to make up a happy little party. After all, we aren't very different from Harley Street, which charges you and me five guineas and Lord This or That a hundred guineas."

Bray was forced to admit himself beaten, but he did not press the matter.

"If you have any doubts," went on Budge, following up his advantage, "I suggest you speak to the people themselves. Miss Mumby and Mr Winterton, for instance, would put in their own words what I have just been telling you."

VII

Charles on his part was doing a little investigation. One name on Bray's list of the guests from whom the Budges were exacting tribute had puzzled him. "Now what is lovely Mrs Walton doing in that crowd?" he thought. He decided he must have a talk with her, and drifted slowly towards the little room known as the drawing-room, in which he had heard Mrs Walton was sitting.

He was about to drift out again when he saw a stranger with Mrs Walton, but his blank stare was transformed to a start of semi-recognition. He jammed in his eyeglass. "Hello, Addington," he said. Charles, whose *métier* as a gossip-writer it had been to know everyone slightly, knew St Clair Addington well.

"Oh, I never realized you knew my fiancé!" exclaimed Mrs Walton cordially.

"Fancy your being in this den of thieves," remarked Addington. "You didn't do the deed, by any chance? I never trust these journalists."

Charles realized that tact and criminal investigation do not go together. Instead of retiring gracefully, he drew his chair into the circle and talked. And while he talked he watched.

At the finish Charles was frankly puzzled. Mrs Walton was in love with Addington, so much was very plain, and Addington, the pious and darling son of the Law Lord whose onslaughts on the second revised Prayer Book had split the Church of England in twain, was completely bewitched by that throaty voice and that shepherdess pink and whiteness. Charles, on the whole, preferred something a little more fine drawn… Charles realized with a start that it was an ominous sign when he thought of another girl when talking to anything so charming as Mrs Walton.

But Mrs Walton was afraid, desperately afraid. When she looked at St Clair, her eyes sparkled, but when she looked away there was a hunted thing peering out, and it cowered as if it was hard pressed.

All three went in to dinner together, and sat at the same table. Worry apparently did not affect Mrs Walton's appetite. She ate with the natural, unaffected gusto which Charles maintained was the glory of true womanliness. But she crumbled her bread and jiggled her cutlery with the incessancy of long-repressed nerves. What with one thing and another, Charles was puzzled. "Perhaps I am a complete ass after all," he sighed resignedly to himself…

Afterwards he dropped into Bray's rooms, on the edge of Chelsea, for a drink. They discussed the case from every angle, but Charles reserved his bombshell for the last.

"By the way, Bray," he said at the door. "You'd better watch Budge. Since this murder he's locked his door and window at night and carried a revolver in his pocket during the day. If you aren't careful you'll have his murder on your hands as well."

"I only hope they don't murder him before I succeed in hanging him," replied Bray grimly.

Chapter Twelve

BUDGE VERSUS BRAY:
CHARLES INTERVENING

At one a.m. that night, or rather, next morning, the curious observer might have seen a long dressing-gown and carpet slippers creeping down the corridors of the hotel. Enveloped in the dressing-gown and peering over the collar was Charles.

Nothing is more difficult of accomplishment than moving quietly at night. Charles, as he overturned the second chair in twenty yards, realized that he needed a great deal of practice in the technique of his art if he were to become a criminal investigator. Very cautiously he crept down the stairs from his floor to the first floor. Suddenly he stepped on something soft. It wriggled, and Charles felt a sensation like five wasp stings on his bare skin. He and the cat screamed together, and he fell down the flight with a series of thuds.

He waited for ten minutes, mopping his scratched ankle and cursing silently. But apparently the residents in the Garden Hotel slept the sleep of the just. He felt his way to Mrs Salterton-Deeley's suite and entered.

Behind the bedroom door the lady snored decorously. Charles switched on the reading-lamp and looked around him. Mrs Salterton-Deeley shared the untidiness of her sex. Her hat lay on the sofa, her coat was thrown over the arm of a chair, and her handbag and gloves were on the bureau. Charles took up her bag and shot the contents on the table. One object only he examined, and then shot it back into the bag with the rest.

"So far, so good," he said to himself. "My theory seems to have been sound."

His next visit was to Mr Winterton's room. Here a quick search located the goal of his investigation in a chest of drawers. His search of Miss Mumby's rooms was more prolonged, but he ran to earth something that satisfied him in one of the lady's shoes—a beautifully brocaded pair which looked as if they had never been worn.

In neither case did he remove anything, but he went back to his cold bed satisfied and slept the sleep of the completely righteous.

II

Charles turned up at Bray's office next day and parked himself in the only comfortable chair with an air of permanency.

"About Budge's alibi," said Charles.

Bray looked up.

With maddening deliberation the other paused while he placed his monocle on the edge of the desk, and with a deft push sent it spinning to the limit of its lanyard. "I believe I could break that," he murmured.

"Good," said the detective sarcastically. "That would be sweet of you."

Charles went on unheedingly. "Now here's a case where I can be useful to you. Hampered as you are by red tape, you cannot take the fairly obvious steps necessary to prove that the Mumby bird and old what's-his-name are liars. I can, with your co-operation."

"How can I co-operate? I am all eagerness," said Bray, unimpressed. "It is not often that Scotland Yard has the chance of helping a brilliant amateur of your gifts."

Charles smiled. "I only want you to lock up Budge."

The detective gaped. "Only! On what charge?"

"Any old charge," the other replied cheerfully. "He probably hasn't a licence for his revolver."

"Don't be a fool, Charles. You know perfectly well that we can't throw people into prison on the offchance of what will follow."

The other dropped his air of gaiety and became serious. "Look here, Bray, I'm not joking. I can't tell you what is in my mind because my way of dealing with the situation isn't going to be strictly legal. But if you can get Budge here and give the impression that he is arrested, I guarantee that I can dispose of that alibi which has caused you so many sleepless nights."

Inspector Bray scratched his head and thought deeply. At last he spoke. "Look here, I disclaim all responsibility for the whole business in advance. But I have been impressed by one or two hits you have made in this case, and I'm ready to admit that in certain points the outsider has advantages over the Yard. We shall send for Budge and ask him to come here to answer a few questions—of his own free will, of course—and it is up to you to make as much or little of it as you please."

Charles grinned. "Good boy. I'm on. Send as early as you can and stand by for developments."

Bray watched him jump to his feet and hurry out, not without a certain amount of misgiving. Eventually he shrugged his shoulders philosophically. He devoted his attention to clearing up his desk.

III

Bray's voice was cooingly polite as he rang up Budge and asked if he would come to Scotland Yard to answer a few questions. Budge willingly agreed, and ten minutes later a Scotland Yard Invicta drew up at the door, and two policemen arrived. A timid chambermaid peeped out at them and saw them escorting Budge with exaggerated cordiality, one each side, to the car. Budge looked uneasy.

The little chambermaid came from a home where such visits were not unknown. She fled down the stairs to the kitchen, where the head waiter was engaged in solemn conference with the cook. He frowned at her as she burst into the room, but her news buoyed her up and onwards.

"Mr Budge has been arrested," she screamed.

"Nonsense, you little fool," said the head waiter automatically.

"He has, he has. Two coppers came and pinched him in the hall—didn't give him time to collect anything even, they didn't."

"Don't jump to conclusions," her immediate superior rebuked her loftily. "He has been consulted by the police and has gone over to the Yard to give evidence."

"Ow, I didn't know that," answered the chastened girl. "I thought as 'ow they'd pinched him, coming the way they did."

"Well, keep yourself under better control," replied the other, and going upstairs to the Budges' room, he rapidly got together all the movable property he could find that seemed valuable. In spite of his calming words, he foresaw the imminent collapse of the Garden Hotel.

I V

"Hello, Colonel," said Charles gaily as he blew into the hotel. "You're just in time to hear a red-hot exclusive story before it's phoned through. Budge has been arrested for the murder of his good lady."

Cantrip whitened. "Arrested? Surely you're joking, Venables!"

"It's a fact. Two burly officers of the law came and whisked him off, and you won't see him again unless you can squeeze into the Old Bailey."

Cantrip showed no surprise, but he showed great irritation. His veined hands stole to his ragged moustache and tugged it nervously. "It's most inconsiderate," he moaned; "how will the hotel be run without him?"

"How, indeed?" asked Charles cheerfully. "Supplies running low, what?" He winked.

Cantrip started. "Good Lord, I didn't realize that you were—" He broke off expressively.

"Even so, I am," answered Charles mendaciously.

"H'm, h'm," boomed the Colonel, worrying his moustache. "I feel so helpless after all these years. We must have a chat about this matter later. Yes, we must have a chat." And the Colonel strode away, deep in thought.

At lunch that day Charles was late. But he had time to see Viola before the gong sounded.

"Look here, Viola," he whispered, "things are breaking. Scotland Yard has invited Budge over to answer some questions, but I want the rumour to go round that he has been arrested—mind, not a soul must know otherwise at lunch."

"Right oh, Charles. This sounds most exciting. You can rely upon me to back you up. I shall swear I saw the warrant, if necessary."

Whatever the nature of the business that made Charles late for lunch, it took him to the rooms of Miss Mumby and Winterton, and this time he abstracted the small objects for which he had searched the night before. He went in to lunch with both in his pockets, and calmly met the eyes of his unconscious victims.

"A bad business," remarked Charles in a loud voice. "I hear from a friend in Scotland Yard that the fellow's confessed."

The head waiter looked staggered, and a waitress dropped a knife with a clatter.

"Goodness knows what will happen here," Charles went on.

The case was discussed from every angle—why, when and how.

"I cannot understand it," said Miss Mumby, turning to Charles and mechanically stroking the kitten which sat with its paws on her bread plate. "I understand that the police view was that it was impossible for Mr Budge to have done it, because both Mr Winterton and myself saw him just about the time of the murder. I don't trust that young man Bray," she went on darkly. "I believe he's looking for someone to fix it on, and he's chosen Mr Budge."

Miss Geranium had been nervously crumbling her bread. Miss Hectoring looked at her once or twice with anxious affection in her eye. Suddenly Miss Geranium rose to her feet. The chair fell backwards with a clatter.

"Hypocrites," she cried passionately.

Charles could not help smiling at the unanimity with which the serried rows of munching jaws stopped dead, and the eyes of everyone flashed nervously in her direction.

"Hypocrites. The curse of the Lord is coming upon you all, you unworthy sinners! Repent before it is too late! Oh, dear—" She collapsed and burst into long, shuddering sobs.

Miss Hectoring tried vainly to calm her. Miss Sanctuary hurried to her side. "There, there, my dear," she soothed. "You mustn't let these things upset you."

Miss Geranium's sobbing died away. "You're a good woman," she murmured.

Charles, sitting a few feet away, could hear Miss Sanctuary's protesting "Nonsense."

"Yes, you are," insisted the other, "too good to be in this den of vice!"

"You're a little feverish, dear," said Miss Sanctuary, feeling her forehead. "Come upstairs and lie down." She drew Miss Geranium to her feet and led her out of the room, her eyes still glittering wildly.

There was an embarrassed silence.

"I will not stand that woman," shouted the Colonel savagely. "I will not, I——" His voice died to a protesting murmur.

"I really think she should be in an asylum, poor soul," whispered Mrs Salterton-Deeley to her neighbour, Mr Nicholas Twing, at the other end of the room. "It would really be far kinder."

Unfortunately, Mrs Salterton-Deeley's whisper was of the penetrating kind. It reached Miss Hectoring, and she plunged like a lion—a sea lion, perhaps—to the defence of her friend.

"I'll tell you something, Mrs Salterton-Deeley," she said, advancing to her table. (Mr Twing's eyes twinkled with amusement, but he gave his whole attention to his food as if to dissociate himself entirely from his table companion.) "Before you're much older, you'll end in an asylum too. Look at your spoon, trembling like a leaf."

Mrs Salterton-Deeley attempted to quell her with a glance. The soup in her spoon, arrested in mid-air, slopped over the sides. Miss Hectoring, glowering like a bulldog, stopped there long enough to make the red-haired woman drop her eyes. Then she left.

As soon as the door was closed, Mrs Salterton-Deeley tittered. No one else laughed.

At another table fragments of a conversation between Eppoliki and Mrs Walton drifted Charles's way. The Egyptian's one good eye rolled wildly. "Maybe a human hand killed Mrs Budge," he said, "maybe not. But what you call the motive force, the striking power—that was some ill deed, perhaps in the poor lady's past, who knows?"

"Do you believe in reincarnation?" asked Miss Arrow tonelessly. She had come in to see Mrs Walton, whom she had met when she stayed at the hotel, and had stayed on to lunch.

Miss Arrow gazed wearily at Eppoliki. She was never animated at the best of times. She smiled her way through life, frail but efficient, with her small, pale, plain face and her waxen skin, forbidding sympathy by her manner before it was offered. She made no advances; she asked for no friendship; she dwelt perpetually in the contemplation of the unwelcome guest which waxed fat unceasing in the delicate fabric of her flesh. Radium, X-rays and surgery might retard its growth, but the day would come when, like the ivy on the wall, it would bring down in ruin its host and protector. Already the unearthly beeswax transparency of the cancer subject had invaded her cheeks. Miss Arrow, thought Charles, made one wonder whether society's pursuit of the murderer was not excessively theatrical and romantic. Jack the Ripper slayed his tens, Cancer and T.B. their tens of thousands...

"Oh, yes, it is an established fact," answered Eppoliki vaguely. (Charles imagined him answering some of his examination questions with similar brevity and finality.) "You all believe in the power of evil, whatever you say. Recently I want a good leather case, value, say, thirty-five shillings. I say to Miss Mumby, 'You buy me a new case, or I put a curse on you.' She got me the case," Eppoliki concluded triumphantly.

"That's blackmail, Eppoliki," said Miss Arrow laughingly.

Mrs Walton shivered. Her lids dropped over her eyes as if the conversation bored her.

"Miss Mumby credulous lady, perhaps," said Eppoliki, "but it is true what I tell you. The hand holds the dagger, the brain conceives the plan, but by our evil past it is aimed and stabbed." He thought a moment. "I do not think Mr Budge commit the murder."

"I feel as if I were living in a madhouse," groaned Viola to Charles under her breath.

"Just let me clear up this case," whispered back Charles, "and I will take you out of it."

"Is that a proposal?"

"It wasn't meant as one, but I'm a man of my word, and if you take it as one, I'll stick to it."

Viola laughed. The noise sounded strange in the dining-room.

V

In a comfortable sitting-room in Scotland Yard, Budge's annoyance was rising to fever heat. After being whirled through the streets of London at top speed in the Invicta, as if they were in pursuit of a car bandit, he had been kept waiting for nearly two hours. It is true that sleek young men with patent-leather hair had been in at frequent intervals to console him, offer him magazines and flute their surprise at the non appearance of a certain Superintendent Chelmsford, but none the less he had waited.

Finally a message had come in to say that Superintendent Chelmsford presented his humblest apologies, but he simply could not be back until half-past two. Inspector Perkins hoped that Mr Budge would kindly lunch with him. Fuming, Budge consented.

Charles did not wait till lunch was over. He slipped upstairs to Winterton's sitting-room and seated himself in an armchair with his back to the door. With his head sunk in his shoulders, no sign of Charles was visible, but no one could say he was actually hiding.

A few minutes later Winterton strolled into the room. He did not look around him, but went straight to the bureau from which Charles had previously extracted the object of his search.

He gave a startled exclamation as he found it missing. He rummaged excitedly through the drawers.

Charles rose silently to his feet. He placed his eye-glass in his eye and his hands in his pocket. "It's no good, Winterton, I know it isn't there, because I've taken it."

Winterton spun round and staggered back. "G-g-good gracious," he said at last, his teeth chattering. "You gave me such a fright. What did you say?"

Charles repeated himself.

Winterton gaped at him for a moment, his mouth opening like that of a fish on dry land. Then he burst into a torrent of abuse. "You thief," he ended. "Give it back at once."

"Oh, no," replied Charles, "you naughty boy! I have confiscated it." He smiled cunningly.

Infuriated, Winterton rushed at him.

Charles placed one hand on Winterton's chest and shot him into the armchair, in which he subsided. "Sit down and no nonsense," he said sternly.

Winterton sat. His eyes gleamed malignantly, and his hands plucked incessantly at the sides of the chair.

"Listen to me, Winterton. I've got your week's supply of heroin here in my pocket. Budge is in jail and you're not going to get any more."

Winterton's voice rose to a protesting whine. "Venables, you can't do that, you can't. You don't realize my sufferings. It's medicine. I must have it." He was a pitiable sight as he bent forward pleading, his eyes fawning like a dog's.

Charles was pitiless. He drew out the small square celluloid box and opened the lid. "H'm, with careful use this would last you a fortnight. And now you haven't a grain."

With an anguished whimper Winterton made a dive at it. Charles firmly shot him back into his chair.

"You beast," whined the bald man.

"Now look here, Winterton," said Charles. "We're going to get the truth from you for a change. You never saw Budge on the night of the murder, did you?"

"No," said the other tonelessly.

"Budge afterwards came to you and pointed out his danger of arrest. No doubt he said it was absolutely false, but he explained to you that if he were arrested, your supply would cease. Like any other addict, you would damn body and soul for your regular shot of dope, and you agreed to repeat the false evidence he made you learn. Am I right?"

"Yes," agreed the other, all fight gone. "What about it?"

"Well, Budge is locked up now. He's confessed. Your source of supply is ended. But I'll give you back your dope if you will sign a statement to the effect that Budge asked you to swear that you had seen him that night, and that without realizing the consequences of your action, you did so."

"I'll sign," said the other, without hesitation. His mind was focussed absolutely on one object. He reached for his precious box.

"Not so fast," replied Charles. "You'll have to wait till I've seen Miss Mumby and got hold of Bray."

Charles went out of the room. As he shut the door he saw Winterton, head bowed forward, fingers plucking nervously at the chair arms.

"Now for the lady. This will need somewhat more delicate handling, but I don't think it will be very difficult."

It wasn't. Charles came out of Miss Mumby's room with a satisfied smile and rang up Bray. Bray was listening to the expostulations of an infuriated Budge—infuriated not without reason, for all that afternoon had been spent with Superintendent Chelmsford. Words cannot paint the extraordinary denseness of Superintendent Chelmsford. Polite—in fact deferentially so—he had gone over every detail with which Budge was concerned, and seemed unable to grasp the simplest point without lengthy explanations. Laboriously, in longhand, with a scratchy nib, he wrote down everything. He insisted on Budge's drawing a plan of the hotel, and then betrayed the greatest difficulty in following him.

Budge's nerves eventually snapped under the strain at a time when even Chelmsford—a magnificent actor—was beginning to perspire slightly from the effort of maintaining an attitude of complete obtuseness. Budge refused to say another word until Bray had arrived, and he then passionately demanded of the Inspector whether he had not already given him all the information for which he was being badgered by Chelmsford.

At that moment the extension telephone in the sitting-room rang, and Charles was put through.

"Hello, Bray. All's well. Come round at once. Budge can be turfed out now, but give yourself twenty minutes' start."

Bray had difficulty in keeping the elation out of his voice as he made a non-committal answer. He found it impossible to believe that Charles had succeeded where he had failed so uncompromisingly, but he was beginning to realize that his lanky junior had a certain natural flair which, for all his lack of training and technique, might avail him where Bray's professional methods would prove useless.

He hurried into the yard and stepped into the Invicta in which Budge had arrived. "The Garden Hotel," he said to the blue-capped constable at the wheel, "and don't waste time."

They plunged into the whirligig of Parliament Square and shot into St James's Park.

VI

Charles met Bray as he came in and took him to one side. "I've done what you wanted," he said. "But you've got to promise me one thing. Don't press Mumby or Winterton as to their motives for their tarradiddles. Stick simply to what you are interested in and turn a blind eye to everything else."

Bray willingly agreed. His second examination of Miss Mumby and Winterton was very different from his first. Broken-spirited and nervous, they readily admitted that they had been prompted in their story by Budge. Bray did not endeavour to press his advantage. He listened to their absurd story without surprise and quickly drew up the statement which they signed. As Winterton affixed his name with trembling fingers, he looked inquiringly at Charles.

"I've put your Christmas presents back where I found them," Charles said.

Pathetically eager, the two rose to their feet and hurried from the room.

"How on earth—" began Bray.

Charles laid his finger to his lips. "Hush," he admonished him dramatically. "There are some things good little detectives should not know. I did it by a combination of blackmail, theft and threats with violence, and I think the less you know about it the better. As Al Capone would say: 'Keep your nose clean.'"

Bray smiled. "Perhaps you're right. I should hate to think what you've been up to, and I'm perfectly ready to believe it's illegal. Anyway, we've got Budge sewn up now. I'll see my boss at once and we shall have a warrant out for him to-morrow. Meanwhile, we'll keep our eye on the hotel in case he tries to forestall us and make a getaway."

"Yes," said Charles reflectively. "I think the next move is to arrest Budge."

He got up and shook himself. "Well, I'll be toddling. I've got to keep the story alive in the *Mercury* somehow. God knows what I can say to-day. Oh, how I wish I could put in the truth!"

Charles hesitated at the door. Then he turned. "Of course," he said, "I'm more than ever certain that Budge is completely innocent."

Before Bray could voice his astonishment the door had closed.

Chapter Thirteen

THE HANGMAN IS ANTICIPATED

M iss Sanctuary was knitting. She glanced up as Mr Budge sat down beside her. The man was plainly agitated about something. "Badly frightened," she thought to herself. She made no remark, however, and the steady click of her needles seemed to reassure him.

He tugged at his tie. "I feel I want some advice," he said at last dryly, not looking at her. "I feel somehow that you could give me the advice I need."

She smiled and took off her spectacles. "You are not the first to say so," she said resignedly, putting them with her knitting in her work-basket. "O. Henry in one of his stories divides people into feet, hands and shoulders. I am afraid I am a shoulder, and to be candid, I rather like it. What is it?"

Budge seemed to have some difficulty in framing his thoughts. "Put it this way," he said warily at last. "Assume a man suspected by the police in connection with this murder. He is innocent, but facts are against him. He believes the murderer must be a relative of a certain person who has a grudge against him." Budge hesitated. "I don't want to make myself out better than I am," he said with an effort. "This grudge was justified in a way. It would definitely harm me if the police knew about it. Yet the only way I could put them on the track of the right person is by telling them the whole story."

Miss Sanctuary was not a fool. She looked at Budge, and without her spectacles, he noticed she had very keen, blue eyes. "If you want my advice, you must be quite candid. Am I right in assuming that you were blackmailing these people and that this was the grudge you talk about?"

Budge wriggled. He had not expected this old lady to make so accurate an estimate of his character. Yet he felt better now that he had voiced the fear that was oppressing his mind. "Well, that's not quite a fair way of putting it," he hedged. "I admit they paid me something for keeping quiet."

"Then in your place," answered Miss Sanctuary, with some distaste, "I should take good care not to tell the police until it became absolutely necessary—in other words, until you are actually arrested."

"You think that, do you?" answered the other, wincing at the word "arrested." "That's what I thought." He looked round apprehensively. "Of course you won't breathe a word to a soul of what I told you?"

"I am not in the habit of making capital of other people's troubles," she answered with a sarcasm that was wasted on him. "I shall not tell anyone else."

When Miss Sanctuary was alone, she carefully replaced her spectacles and resumed her knitting.

"How extraordinary!" she remarked to one of Miss Mumby's cats, which had been an indifferent auditor of the conversation.

II

"What precisely did you mean last night," Bray asked Venables at eleven o'clock next day, "by saying you did not not believe Budge is guilty? You really are a most perplexing bloke. You spend a busy and probably extremely illegal afternoon breaking Budge's alibi and then you tell me you think the fellow is an innocent lamb."

"It is Budge's alibi which for one thing makes me think he was innocent," Charles replied. "We know it was manufactured hastily after the crime, and was full of weaknesses. Now I have a tremendous respect for the fellow's intelligence, and I am quite sure that if he really had planned the murder, he would have arranged for a watertight alibi beforehand. He would never have risked the obvious possibility of the nurse seeing him coming away. The only thing that seems Budge-like is the neat and expeditious disposal of the remains, and I think we are both agreed there's a curious story behind that in which Blood is involved."

"Your reasoning is delightfully subtle," Bray said, laughing. "But if we adopted it we should never get a conviction, because we should feel that all the obvious suspects would never have been such fools as to be suspected. A little more experience, Venables, and you will be amazed at the perpetual folly of criminals. It is a form of egoism which takes the shape of underrating the perception of other people."

"Anyway, it's all an academic matter," answered Charles calmly. "If you arrest Budge, blue ruin will break out here, and out of the wreck we should be able to salve some evidence that will point to the true murderer."

Unfortunately, Budge for the moment was not to be found. He had gone out that day and left no message as to where he was going.

"I expect you gentlemen put the wind up him yesterday," the head waiter told Bray with some relish, and dropping into a more vulgar accent than his usual tone, to show his independence. Budge had returned just as he was rifling a cigar-box in the sitting-room, and the memory of the proprietor's remarks still rankled. "He's probably legged it."

"Did he speak to anyone before he went?" asked Charles.

"Yes, he had a word with Miss Sanctuary."

They sought out Miss Sanctuary, who was peaceably knitting before the fire in the little sitting-room.

"Yes, I spoke to him this morning," she said. "I was telling him about the scene with Miss Geranium yesterday, Inspector. You were there, weren't you, Mr Venables? Poor lady, I am afraid she isn't happy here."

"Did he tell you where he was going, by any chance?"

"No, why?"

The Inspector hesitated. "To tell you the truth, madam, we want him badly." He tapped his breast pocket significantly.

"Dear me," Miss Sanctuary said. "Have you a warrant for his arrest?"

The detective nodded.

"Poor man! Everyone here was saying he had been arrested yesterday. It is all very confusing."

"It was only a rumour yesterday. To-day it's a fact," said the detective grimly.

"Well, I hope you've got the right man at last," Miss Sanctuary said, pausing in her knitting for a moment. "It's an awful thought looking at one's neighbours and thinking that it might have been any of them, must have been one of them, who did this dreadful thing. Only yesterday, when Miss Hectoring came in perfectly white with anger after some words with Mrs Salterton-Deeley, and laid her hand on my arm, I thought that might have been the hand that was pressed against my face on that terrible evening."

She smiled apologetically. "Of course it's all a fancy, but I shall be glad all the same when the matter is settled. I suppose you are sure you're right this time?"

"Certain," Bray assured her.

"The police are absolutely positive," remarked Charles truthfully.

Miss Sanctuary reflected for a moment. "I suppose it is my duty to give you all the help I can," she said at last. "Yet I feel as if it were cruel somehow to set the police on a fellow-human's track. Not that I do not admire the great work you do," she added quickly.

Bray waited.

"While I was with him I heard him speak to someone on the phone and say he would be in at the East Kensington Junior Liberal Club between two and three," she said at last. "I suppose if you go there you'll be able to serve your warrant."

"This is very good of you," said Bray. "You needn't feel sorry about it. It is only a matter of time before we get our man, you know. The information you have given us makes practically no difference."

Miss Sanctuary smiled gratefully. "Thank you. Still, I do not think one ought to shirk any responsibility that justly belongs to one. I gave my little terrier, Tim, poison with my own hands the other day when he caught spinal meningitis. It was kinder than letting a vet give it, I think, and I think I would have much less compunction in bringing to justice the murderer of the kind lady that we all loved in this hotel."

The two rose to their feet.

"I am afraid the whole sorry tale is not yet done, Miss Sanctuary," said Charles gravely. "If my premonitions are correct, we shall all have had a shock or two more before we can say the chapter is ended."

III

"I've been looking everywhere for you, Inspector," Blood remarked, going up to the pair with a worried look. "What's all this about Budge being arrested yesterday? I saw him this morning walking round without a hair out of place."

"They only asked him up to Scotland Yard to question him yesterday, Blood," answered Charles, "but the rumour was an anticipation of the truth. Bray is looking for him now with a warrant for his arrest for the wilful murder of his wife."

"Are you certain he is guilty?"

"You are the second person who has asked me that question within five minutes," the detective replied wearily. "Do you think we arrest people out of pique?"

Blood ignored the mild sarcasm. "Come up to my room for a moment. I have something of real urgency to tell you."

There was a note of tension in his voice. Bray followed him without demur. Charles was about to drop discreetly back when Blood turned to him. "You'd better come too, Venables. You can confirm one or two points in my story."

Blood seated the two in his room, and talked aimlessly for a little. His voice was strained, and his eyes were roving. Bray recognized the symptoms. A confession was coming.

"I have a statement to make," said the parson abruptly. He clasped his hands together till the knuckles whitened. "It was I who dismembered the body of Mrs Budge."

Bray said nothing. Several queries suggested themselves, but, taught by experience, he ruthlessly suppressed them. Charles nodded his head sagely. His eyeglass flashed.

Blood was speaking again in a strained, dry voice. "I am, of course, innocent of the murder, but I dared not speak before till my suspicions were corroborated by your action in charging Budge. Oh, it was a monstrous folly and I have paid the penalty of it a thousand times over in regret and sleeplessness, but it's easy to be wise after the event."

The detective made an inarticulate noise of agreement. And in truth the little parson looked as if he had endured enough. The veins stood out beneath his eyes and his lips were drawn with worry.

"Not maniples
Nor all the gorgeous vestments of the East
Shall medicine thee again to that sweet sleep
Which thou owedst yesterday,"

misquoted Charles to himself irrelevantly.

"Venables was in the room," he went on, "when I lifted the lid of the laundry basket to put in my dirty collar. There, staring up at me, was the face of Mrs Budge, distorted with *rigor mortis* and the *rictus* supervening on death by strangulation. My nerve snapped, I suppose, but it did not feel like that. It felt as if my brain had suddenly cleared. I felt something in me say in a whisper, *'Keep it quiet, or you'll hang!'* I didn't really mean to keep it quiet then, only to get time to think. And then Budge came into the room and wanted to empty the basket. I knew then that he had put the body there, and suddenly it came to me that the sly devil had invented some story which would involve me hopelessly, which might hang me or, at the best, cloud my name for ever."

He paused. The sweat stood out on his forehead and brimmed his eyebrows. "I bundled them both out of the room and then locked the door. You must remember that my medical training has made me what you might describe as callous about these things. That wasn't Mrs Budge lying there, her face a caricature of mortality. The real woman had already faced her Maker, and the basket held only her cast-off body."

Blood paused reflectively. He was living the scene over again. "One is never what one expects to be like at these moments. I played for quite a time with the idea of the cast-off body, the dirty clothing of the spirit, lying in that laundry basket, and which I was going to dispose of with as little ceremony as you would an incriminating bundle of clothing. I thought it would make a good metaphor for a sermon, a thought old Donne would have delighted in. Then I got to work... It were as if I was back in my medical student days... I made a neat job of it, and carried the pieces down as I had opportunity in the little attaché-case everybody is used to seeing me carry about. It was absurdly simple. Then I cleaned up scrupulously, and when an opportunity offered itself, exchanged the laundry basket, which I felt might still have some traces of its contents, for the clean one in Budge's room... I felt quite safe until you talked about searching the room, and then I threw Mrs Budge's shawl, which I still had, and the scalpels, out of the window. I had not had time to get rid of these before the first discoveries were made."

Bray smiled. "We saw you throwing them out of the window, and Charles had already interpreted your consternation on that morning, so your story does not come as altogether a surprise to us."

"Oh, of course, I've been every sort of a fool," the parson answered shamefacedly. "I've gone out of my way to implicate myself and shield the real murderer—all because of a moment's panic. I'm a disgrace to my cloth, and I suppose I shall have to stand my trial as accessory."

"We should certainly be justified in making you do so," said Bray, "but if we call you as witness for the prosecution we may overlook it, in view of your voluntary statement."

"It will be treating me better than I deserve," said the other humbly. "I feel like Christian when he lost his burden."

Charles was staring at his nails with a baffled look. Bray knew why he was baffled, for Bray was equally puzzled himself. It was incredible that any human being of intelligence would act as Blood had done, on the face of it. Blood was keeping something back—there were some incriminating circumstances which had made Blood feel that the police would suspect him of the murder and give them a prima facie case against him.

Why was he keeping it back? And would it be worth pressing him or would it only give the defence an added weapon with which to attack Blood? For Bray saw that they would make the most of Blood's suspicious actions to discredit the Crown's case.

Suddenly inspiration, luminous and clear, came to him, as it comes all too rarely to the struggling criminal investigator. He rose to his feet, trying to suppress his elation. "Did you have much job to get out the bloodstains afterwards?" he said carelessly.

"No," replied the other. "There weren't many. All of the blood, except that in some of the major vessels, had congealed."

Bray shot at him a look charged with significance and paused meaningly. "I suppose you used some of that patent cleanser of your own invention?" he said at last.

As Blood absorbed the full meaning of the words he wilted. White to the lips, he collapsed in his chair. Charles watched him incredulously.

"No doubt I'm dense," remarked Charles bitterly when they were in the corridor, "but why—oh, why—did our boy friend curl up and die at the mention of patent cleansers?"

Bray had the cutting in his wallet. He fished it out and told the other how he had found it in the envelope Mrs Budge had put in her solicitor's safe keeping. "In one of those flashes of intuition one occasionally gets," he explained, "I placed Blood as the most likely man to fill the rôle of the young swindler. He did not dare expose Budge because of the hold Budge had over him."

The detective paused a minute reflectively. "I still cannot understand why Budge did not make use of his hold over Blood to blackmail him. I feel as if, although I've got the solution in my hands, I'm not holding it the right way up."

Charles thumped him joyously on the back. "Hooray, the missing link!" he exclaimed. "I see it all now. Bray, my boy, in a short time I shall such a tale unfold as will freeze the youthful marrow of your bones."

"I am glad it's so simple," the other said irritably. "It's as clear as mud to me."

IV

Bray discovered that the East Kensington Junior Liberal Club took a bit of finding. Here a fresh annoyance awaited him. He went straight to the barman as the prime source of information. The barman, a melancholy soul, gaped at Bray's official card.

"Mr Budge has been and gorn," he said. "There was a letter for him marked *Urgent*, and he read it and hurried out."

Bray was about to hurry out when the barman called him back.

"Hi, mister," he called.

Bray returned. Some subterranean convulsion seemed to shake the barman, and an expression of extreme cunning screwed up his eyes and mouth.

"He knows you're after him," said the man at last. "Someone's tipped him the word."

The barman's face now assumed an even more portentous expression. An enormous wink reduced the length of one side of his face by about half an inch.

"It was that letter," the barman remarked diffidently. "I suppose a sight of the letter would be worth something to you, eh?"

The detective saw daylight. No doubt a threat would produce the letter, but he preferred to pay his way. He produced a pound note and exchanged it without difficulty for a crumpled piece of paper. Its contents gave him an acute pang.

"DEAR MR BUDGE,—The police hold a warrant for your arrest for the murder of your wife. Your conviction is almost certain.

"I am taking the great risk of telling you this and warning you that the police are coming to the Club to serve the warrant. I have got together a few clothes and all the cash that was in your desk and have put them in a bag which you will find in the toolshed in the garden. Take it, but for heaven's sake, hurry.

"I believe you may be guilty. I am, I suppose, a malefactor in the eyes of the law in helping you. But I must, now that I have the opportunity, register my little protest against the cruel and vindictive laws of this country, that take God's prerogative out of His hand and wield it mercilessly, revengefully, hatefully. While this canker of capital punishment exists, I must, and shall, range myself against the institutions that permit it.

"If I have saved you from death, repay it with a better life. The best of us are sinners. Burn this.

"LAURA SANCTUARY."

Stupefied with astonishment for a moment, Bray hesitated. "The old fox!" he muttered. Yet this was not the first time he had encountered the militancy of the humanitarian. The anti-vivisectionist and he to whom the flesh of animals is taboo can offend more outrageously than the man who merely sins because he has a mind to. Conscience doth make heroes of us all.

Then he sprang to the phone. Speaking to his Chief, he secured at once the necessary arrangements to prevent Budge leaving the Channel ports, or Lympne, Croydon and Heston airports.

Then he jumped into a taxi, but he realized that Budge had quite two hours' start.

V

The toolshed was a melancholy, wooden structure at the bottom of the garden. The tarred fabric on the roof was peeling off, and cobwebs and dust almost completely prevented any ray of light from penetrating the window to the interior.

He opened the door warily. Coming from the sunlight into the shade, he could only see dimly, but he could make out the figure of a man in the corner staring at him.

"Is that you, Budge?" he asked.

There was no answer.

Bray fished out his matches and struck one.

No earthly officer of the law would ever caution Budge. No earthly tribunal would sit in judgment of the fact or of the law upon him. A rope was wrapped once round his neck and twice round the rafters and his feet were off the ground. Anticipating the defter attention of an official hand, he had hanged by the neck until dead...

Quarter of an hour later, when the machine of the law was grinding, with this new development in the hopper, Bray was uncertain whether to be glad or sorry. He looked again at the shaky handwriting, shaky no doubt with the contemplation of the extremity of death.

It began:

"TO THE CORONER.

"I learned to-day that a warrant was out for my arrest for the murder of my wife. I thought at first I should make a bolt for it, but what's the good? Even if I got away clear—and that's more than anyone wanted for murder has done before me—what sort of life should I lead with the thought of that terrible evening always before me?

"I was a fool. I was mad. The verdict is suicide while of unsound mind, Mr Coroner, and the verdict on my wife at the adjourned inquest is, 'Murdered by her husband, George Budge.'"

"Extraordinarily helpful and considerate," remarked Charles, reading over his shoulder. "How did he do it, by the way?"

"The orthodox way," answered the detective. "He stood on this box and adjusted this rope. Then he kicked the box away. Primitive, but effective."

"Well, what do you think about it?" asked Charles.

"We seem to have reached the end of the most tangled case in my experience," Bray replied. "There is always a slight element of chance about a conviction by a judge and jury. Now Budge has convicted himself—judge and jury and executioner in one."

"Y'know, Bray," remarked Charles, "I must confess that you've been right more often than I've thought."

"A handsome admission from the amateur," the detective said, smiling.

"Yes," went on the other remorselessly. "For instance, you laid down at the beginning of the investigation that a murderer never commits suicide."

Bray had the grace to look shamefaced. "There are exceptions to every rule of human conduct," he admitted.

"I don't agree. I still believe you're right."

The detective looked at him incredulously. "Really, Charles, you push subtlety too far. Are you suggesting this is not a case of suicide? What facts have you to support such an extraordinary idea? Or don't you feel the need for facts?"

"My main quarrel with Budge's suicide is that if it is a suicide the elaborate theory I have carefully formulated falls to the ground," said Charles seriously.

Bray raised his eyebrows in mock alarm. "My dear fellow, why didn't you tell me before? I will see that that point of view is put to the Coroner."

Charles waved his monocle deprecatingly. "Have the goodness not to be sarcastic," he said plaintively. "I'd far rather see someone swatting flies with a garden roller than a policeman being sarcastic... Where was I? Oh, yes. Suicide doesn't fit in with my theory. Again, I am prepared to swear on stylistic evidence that this letter has not been written by Budge."

"Stylistic evidence!" exclaimed the detective. "My hat!"

"Yes, of course, it seems funny to you," retorted Charles disgustedly. "How typical of the police attitude to evidence! You will recognize a science of graphology, but not one of literary criticism. You accept physical alibis that are based on the evidences of witnesses, and therefore whose truth is dependent entirely on the psychological make-up of your witnesses, but you will not accept moral alibis that are based on a first-hand study by psychiatrists of the psychological make-up of the accused. All right! If you won't accept my expert evidence as a literary critic, go to your pet graphologist. I don't know a thing about that particular quackery, but if this is anything more than a passable imitation of the handwriting of Budge, I'll eat my hat."

"We should give the letter to a graphologist as a matter of course," replied Bray, who had not, in fact, intended to do anything of the sort. "How and why do you suggest Budge was murdered—or perhaps you think it was an accident?"

"I believe Budge was murdered by whomever he was so afraid of that he locked his door and carried a revolver," was the answer. "The suicide is a very clumsily planned one, because if, as I am certain, that confession is a forgery, a moment's thought should have shown the murderer that there was a distinct danger of its being discovered."

"Why kill him, anyway?" asked the detective. "Is there any need to anticipate the hangman?"

"Presumably there is, and such a possibility squares with the theory I have in mind. The whole murder was very hastily planned, and I should imagine the murderer met Budge going out of the toolshed. Either he could not stop him escaping, or else he was afraid that Budge would ultimately fall into your hands. I suspect the latter was the case, and that the murderer was afraid that when Budge was faced with the capital charge, he would release information which would implicate the real murderer. Budge may even have known the murderer all the time. In that case Budge's doom was sealed directly his arrest was decided upon, and Miss Sanctuary's intervention only altered the scene of the murder without precipitating it.

"As I visualize it, the murderer hastily decided on his plan of action and prepared the forged confession. Then he tracked his victim down, following him to the toolshed, a most convenient place for his purpose. Here he murdered him and staged the scene well enough to take in Scotland Yard."

Bray looked sceptical. "If he is as enterprising as you say, he almost deserves his freedom. At any rate it looks as if he has finished up my case nicely with no loose ends. I must point out that before you expect me to believe this story you might be a little clearer yourself on the motive that made Budge's death so urgent a matter that it could not be left to the professional attention of the common hangman."

Charles shrugged his shoulders. "Have you found the pencil with which this letter was written?" he asked.

Bray opened a felt-padded box, and grinned maliciously. "Yes, here it is—a perfect thumb and forefinger print of the deceased," he said. "Sorry!"

Charles's eye brightened. Jamming in his monocle he bent over the pencil and examined it closely. "Excellent," he murmured, "excellent! If the unknown genius who planned this affair had ever seen Budge writing he wouldn't have made this error."

"Why? Was he left-handed? I've never come across such a case."

"No, but he held a pencil or pen so that the shaft, instead of passing between the forefinger and thumb, passes between the forefinger and the second finger. In this position the pencil is guided by both these fingers and the thumb, but it is mainly the second finger and the thumb that do the work, and it is their prints which you would expect to predominate. I should say that on a thick pencil like this it would be impossible for anyone who writes like Budge to leave a print like this.

"I noticed that Budge wrote like this more than another person would have done," he went on, "because I do so myself. It is not an uncommon habit, and my own theory is that it is less tiring to the hand. It is possible for anyone who holds a pencil in the normal way to write in this unorthodox way, but on the other hand, if you are used to holding it between the forefinger and the second finger, one can make no sort of progress at all with the orthodox grip."

Bray was plainly impressed after Charles had demonstrated what he meant. It was the sort of minor detail which by its very unimportance appealed to his trained brain. A few more of these and he admitted that he would begin to attach some weight to Charles's fantastic theory.

"Anyway, get your graphologist busy," Charles went on, "and keep your mind open, that's all I ask. For the moment, and from the journalistic standpoint, this is going to be made to look like a suicide. It's a lovely story and all the better when it comes out at the inquest that the police suspect foul play, thanks to the brilliance and brains of the (now) star crime expert of the *Mercury*, one Charles Venables."

Bray smiled unenthusiastically.

Charles, however, did not wait for any comment, but peered round the toolshed. "There's one thing I can't understand," he remarked when he returned to Bray's side. "I can't quite see how Budge allowed himself to be hanged without some sort of a struggle, and there's no sign of one here. I can only suggest that he was surprised and stunned. It must have needed a fairly hefty blow to make him unconscious for long enough to stage this scene."

Bray's answer was interrupted by the police doctor who pulled the detective aside.

"The cause of death is undoubtedly strangulation due to hanging. There is one point I cannot quite account for." The doctor removed his pince-nez and stared at Bray as if he would see the answer to the problem written across his chest. "Yes, it's rather puzzling," he repeated. "There is a definite contusion on the cranium, with severe extravasation. It looks as if the fellow had either bumped his head violently or was hit there not long before he died. Unless his skull is exceptionally thick, I should have expected it to lay him out."

Bray looked at Venables wordlessly. He grinned. "I hate to admit it, Charles, but it looks as if you're right."

Chapter Fourteen

THE SECRET OF THE GARDEN HOTEL

"The honours of the day are with you, Charles," admitted Bray, as they drank a coffee the next morning and reviewed the case. "Our graphologist reports that the confession is a fairly clumsy forgery of Budge's handwriting. That, together with the medical evidence and your own observation about the finger-prints on the pencil, will certainly give us a verdict of 'Wilful Murder' at the inquest."

Bray's cordiality had survived even the strain of Charles's splash in the *Mercury*. Charles had crept from the position of "Special Correspondent" to that of initials, but to-day the *Mercury* had blossomed out with his full name and portrait inset in his "story." Charles was at the peak of his professional career, one might say, without undue sarcasm, while Bray was distinctly on the down-grade.

There had been a certain tinge of frost in Olympian voices that morning, and Bray, who was scrupulously honest in certain matters, had not improved his position by giving Charles—an outsider—the fullest credit for a true appreciation of Budge's apparent suicide.

"There's a murderer walking loose in that hotel," his Chief had said. "Good heavens, Bray, you must have some suspicion. In all my professional career I have never known a case of an inside job where the detective in charge did not at least have a pretty shrewd guess as to where the trouble lay. This fellow, Blood, now! His actions positively reek with suspicion. He's confessed to one felony.

Don't, for heaven's sake, neglect the obvious. God help us when Scotland Yard tries to reason like Sherlock Holmes."

"Unfortunately," Bray had replied, "Blood had been sitting with Lady Viola for the whole of the time during which the second murder could possibly have been committed." Viola, who knew Blood's part in the tragedy and felt quite ill, she said, when she spoke to him, had been forced to hear the parson meander on about the Coptic rite with Eppoliki, and had only endured it because he had started out by giving her studio a useful order for copying and adapting some vestments from an old illuminated missal. Her professional conscience had made her listen to the subsequent discussion, and there was Blood, reflected Bray gloomily, with a first-class alibi. It was so good and so artificial that it was in itself suspicious, but heavens, thought the detective, he was falling into the very subtlety that his Chief had condemned.

"Let's start at the beginning, Charles," he groaned at last. "Motive—blackmail. We know the people who are being black-mailed. Who had the means? and in which case was the secret such that they dare not let the blackmailer fall into the hands of the police?"

The journalist was silent for a moment. "Can you stand a sudden shock?" he remarked solicitously at last.

"I think so," said Bray wonderingly. "I could stand almost anything after the Commissioner's few terse words this morning. I suppose you are going to confide in me as to how you frightened Winterton and Miss Mumby into telling the truth. Well, if it will help my case, for the Lord's sake tell me."

"Well, the surprise is this. Your select little list of people who are being blackmailed is, I am afraid, quite useless. Winterton, Miss Mumby, Mrs Salterton-Deeley, Twing, Cantrip, Mrs Walton and Miss Geranium are all as innocent of paying hush-money as I am. They have never paid a cent of blackmail in their lives."

"Oh, my God," groaned the detective. "I've passed the stage where your most astounding assertions can leave me incredulous. I feel like Alice must have felt after the first two or three hours in Wonderland. I should like to venture one or two humble observations, all the same. If they are not being blackmailed, why did the good people you mentioned subsidize the Budges to the tune of several thousands a year?"

Charles smiled. Settling himself in his chair, he stirred his coffee. "The Garden Hotel is one of the most amazing institutions I have ever heard of. It is only by chance that I have just discovered its secret." He paused, and then went on slowly: "Those people who paid so heavily for the privilege of living in the Garden Hotel got their money's worth. They are dope addicts, and they paid for a regular supply of heroin and other narcotics—£2,000 a year, dope found."

Bray stared at him incredulously. "Surely you are not telling me that people like Winterton and Mrs Salterton-Deeley are addicts. Good heavens, I have had some experience of the tribe and they have none of the stigmata."

"You policemen are incurably romantic," sighed Charles. "The novels of Edgar Wallace should really have been forbidden to anyone below the rank of Commissioner. You are as bad as the temperance cranks who think of everyone who drinks as a beery-breathing, red-nosed, reeling old reprobate. Do you think every drug addict creeps round with staring eyes, pallid face and twitching fingers, in a sort of perpetual delirium tremens?"

Bray grinned. "Most of those who fall into our hands are not unlike your description, allowing for a little journalistic exaggeration."

"That fall into your hands, yes," agreed Charles. "Most drunkards who fall into the hands of the police are of the vicious d.t. type. But just as there are heavy drinkers who can carry their drink like gentlemen, there are addicts who can sniff their dope and still retain a semblance of common humanity."

"Go on," said the detective, weakening. "I'm getting interested. But how do you know so much about this?"

Charles grinned. "When I said recently that I had some previous experience of detective work, I was not pulling your leg. Just after I left Cambridge, a friend of mine there—Xavier Cunningham— you probably know his name—persuaded me to assist him at the International Narcotics Bureau of the League of Nations at Geneva. I was there for two years, and would be there still, only, unfortunately, the job was honorary, and it became necessary for me to earn my living."

The detective regarded his friend with a new respect. He could have sworn that Charles's part in certain phases of the investigation had shown more familiarity with the procedure of criminal investigation than any outsider should have had. It had unsettled him, and now he realized that he had had the assistance of a youngster versed in the most delicate and intricate form of criminal investigation (taking it all in all) that could be found. The lad whom Xavier Cunningham had plucked from Oxford to help him in combating a traffic that ramified from China to Peru must have had a nose for the game. And, of course, Charles's casual manner, the slightly vapid and idiotic grin, formed a perfect "cover" for a job in which the investigator, unlike the police detective, does not work with the power of the law behind it, but often only under sufferance, and sometimes, where the law itself is venal and corrupt, in active opposition to it.

"Story-book amateurs" had been the initial verdict of the Yard on first coming into contact with the slim-waisted, meek-eyed young preciosities with which Xavier Cunningham had surrounded himself. Their verdict had been considerably modified after a little experience of the steel determination beneath the velvet glove, the relentlessness with which a quarry who was started in the bazaars of Calcutta was followed to the Bowery, run close at Stockholm, and finally cornered in Buenos Aires. After a little experience of this, Sûreté and Yard had been glad to co-operate with a "Cunningham's Chick" when it was reasonably possible, and Bray realized that this would take the sting out of the Commissioner's soreness with him for the part Charles had played in the case.

"In the Narcotics Bureau one soon learned there were two types of drug addict. There is the type who has to increase continually the dose in order to extract a fresh sensation from it. The dose required to give him a kick gets bigger and bigger, till he can afford it no longer. Then he 'reforms.' He goes to a nursing-home or special institution, and the dose is whittled down, day by day. It's a mental strain: infinite precautions, and perhaps brute force, are needed to prevent the addict getting hold of supplies while he is being 'cured.' But at last his reformation is complete. The drug has been eliminated from his system.

"He can then start all over again, and gratify his craving at a reasonable cost until the time comes when the dose he must have to satisfy his craving is beyond his means. Then, of course, he reforms again. So the vicious circle goes on till his system cracks, as sooner or later it must."

"Are none of these cures genuine?" asked the detective in surprise.

"Bless your innocence, no!" replied the other. "Not in ninety-nine cases out of a hundred. The desire for the drug never dies. In the Bureau one became fairly familiar with that type of addict. He is the type who falls into your hands when he is in a station of life where he can afford neither a sufficient supply of the drug nor a cure.

"This was where the Budges were so diabolically clever. They chose the second type of addict—the addict that never needs to increase his dose—to all outward appearance normal, law-abiding citizens but rotten to the core inside, with every spark of enterprise and humanity frozen with the drug.

"To these people the Garden Hotel offered a paradise. A comfortable home where their needs were understood and a regular supply of the drug round which their whole lives revolved! Oh, the Budges had picked their clients with care and discrimination! All had a sufficient income to pay the heavy tribute exacted without feeling it. All—while slaves of the drug habit—were of the type whom a constant dose sufficed, and who would show little traces of its ravages in ordinary life. Though the soul was rotten, the façade remained good. There is no task so difficult as to 'spot' such an addict if he is sufficiently careful. Many a pillar of respectability and man of influence and intelligence is secretly dependent for his peace of mind and equanimity on his regular sniff of dope. And here I was, an ex-assistant of Cunningham's, in a den of them for three days before I caught one of them out—Miss Mumby it was—in a surreptitious sniff."

"It certainly makes things clearer," admitted the detective, "but I still find it difficult to reconcile the abnormality with such comparatively normal people."

"I think one could have detected it sooner," replied Charles, "if it had not been for the murder, which produced such a tension in the atmosphere that it was sufficient cause for anyone's odd behaviour. Miss Geranium is a clear case of religious melancholia, aggravated by doping, and all of them have the bright eyes and the small appetite of the 'coke'-sodden physique. Put them in ordinary surroundings, in an ordinary atmosphere, and their strangeness would stick out a mile."

"When did you really become certain?" asked Bray.

"The night before last, when I slipped into Miss Mumby's room and Winterton's and found the little hiding-place where they kept their dope. I saw then how Budge had constructed his alibi. He had gone to them and told them that if he were arrested their supply would dry up. That was enough—he had touched the springs of their existence, and they were prepared to perjure themselves black to keep Budge free. The next day they heard that Budge had been arrested, and when they found that their week's supply of dope had been stolen, they simply caved in. To get it back they would have admitted anything, and so I forced them to admit the truth." Charles grinned brazenly.

"May heaven forgive you," exclaimed the detective. "Larceny, blackmail, and aiding and abetting. It's just as well you refused to tell me anything about it!"

"Yes, isn't it?" agreed Charles. "Of course, the point that interested me as an ex-member of the Narcotics Bureau was where the stuff was coming from. It is the most difficult thing in the world to get a regular illicit supply of narcotics so that you can rely absolutely upon your shipments, yet this was being done in this case. Week after week the residents of the hotel got their week's supply, neatly boxed, and with no incriminating messages or exchange of money. Finally, I picked on Blood. Your revelation of his past gave me the clue. If the Budges had a hold on Blood, they might well keep him at the hotel and blackmail him, not for money, but as a regular source of supply. As a medical man he might not have much difficulty in getting it, but it seemed to me that bacteriology was not a very good cover for a regular order for dope.

"Blood was cleverer than I thought," Charles admitted. "When I found that the titles of three monographs written by him were 'Heroin Immunization,' 'Narcotics and the Amœba,' 'Paralysis and Local Anæsthetics,' I realized he had managed to combine the two successfully. A part of his bacteriological work, at any rate, was carried out deliberately in a field where he could order, without suspicion, large and regular quantities of drugs."

"What an extraordinary story!" commented the Inspector. "I don't think I have ever heard of a case remotely resembling it."

"The Bureau came across something very similar in Monaco," said Charles. "In that case, however, it was a bogus nursing-home, specifically run for curing addicts. No attempt was made to cure them, however. On the contrary, they were kept regularly supplied."

"I don't know that it was altogether a wise move to mix their paying guests with normal individuals," Bray remarked. "Of course, it was sheer bad luck entertaining unawares an angel in the person of an ex-member of the Narcotics Bureau, but bad luck apart, I should have thought it was risky."

"I don't know," said Charles. "I think, on the whole, it was the safest move. People like Lady Viola and Miss Sanctuary and Miss Arrow are so patently nice and pleasant that freaks like Miss Geranium and Eppoliki simply sink into the background as the sort of quaint fauna one does meet in a Kensington hotel."

"I notice that the sheep were only mingled with the goats some time after the show had been running," the detective admitted. "Probably something happened which induced the Budges to camouflage their business a little."

"What I am really interested to know," Charles speculated, "is what the police attitude to the affair is going to be."

Bray thought for a moment. "I shall have to discuss it with the Commissioner, of course, but I fancy we shall drop the matter, beyond keeping an eye on these people. The Garden Hotel will disintegrate now, and the real criminals have met their Nemesis. The law looks with comparative pity on the victims of the narcotic habit. It is the panders that must be made to pay, and here they have already paid the extreme penalty. Blood, we could take action against, of course, but the poor devil was blackmailed, and I fancy he has purged his offence many times over in fear and hate. I can see the greatest difficulty in proving he was the actual channel, too, now that the Budges are dead. No! It seems to me that unless Headquarters have different views, the whole business can be left to liquidate itself."

"I agree with you absolutely," said Charles. "Remains the more important problem—By Whose Hand? The problem is immensely complicated by this new development, in that it supplies a completely new crop of people, all absolutely devoid of moral fibre, and therefore absolutely untrustworthy. At the same time it robs us of the obvious motive, since why should any one of them want to dry up that beneficent source of supply, their *alma mater*, Mrs Budge?"

"Why, indeed? I can't help feeling," grumbled the detective, "that the whole drug business is a red herring which Providence has drawn across the trail on purpose to make a fool of me. I'm damned if I'll sit here speculating myself silly. There are about a hundred new lines on which I can start work, and the sooner I get on to one of them, the better."

Rising to his feet with a jerk, the detective strode off.

I I

Charles poured himself out another cup of coffee. "My beautiful chain of evidence has one weak link," he thought to himself. "Luckily, Bray didn't spot it. That link is Mrs Walton. Poor child, if ever innocence was in any look it is in those misty eyes. She's frightened, horribly frightened of something. Yet she's no more a drug addict than Viola. What the devil could she have been buying with her two thousand a year? If I could find that out, I might be nearer the essential motive."

"Is the coffee so bad, Charles?" asked Viola. "You're scowling at it as if it were a bowl of poison." She dropped into a chair behind him. "What is happening here?" she asked. "This suicide of Budge's—is it the end?"

"Only the beginning, I'm afraid," he answered gravely. "It isn't suicide, it's murder."

Viola listened to his explanation with amazement.

"It seems incredible that one of those people we play cards with, and have our meals with, is a murderer," she said at the end. "Yet that's what it amounts to, doesn't it?"

"It isn't the only thing you are going to find incredible," he answered, and he told her of the secret behind the Garden Hotel, the subtle filaments which bound Blood, the Budges and the guests into one sinister organization.

"Poor creatures," said Viola at the finish. "Well, of course, I knew there was something weird lurking just round the corner all the time. When I went into a room, it was as if the conversation had stopped suddenly and started hurriedly on a new subject. I felt like an interloper—except, of course, with Miss Arrow and Miss Sanctuary—and Mrs Walton."

"Yet somehow or other, Mrs Walton is on the other side of the fence," said Charles. "She doesn't dope, but yet she was in the grips of the Budge organization."

"I can't understand it," Viola answered, shaking her head. "She is essentially nice, and although she keeps me a little at arm's length, I think she is delightful."

"So do I."

Viola smiled. "You needn't be quite so hearty," she teased him. "I shall begin to feel a little jealous."

"Don't trifle with me," he said sternly. "My heart is thine. Mock me not. There is no more susceptible time than twelve o'clock in the morning, when one has just got up and one's vitality is at its lowest ebb. It ill becomes you to put on that fetching little chain dog-collar and torment me with unrequited pangs."

Viola smiled. "I had a frantic telegram from my father this morning. He's just realized that this Garden Hotel, which has been in the headlines of the papers for the last week, is the one at which I am staying."

"Highly undesirable," the Earl had wired, "stay Garden Hotel while murder stop Suggest move Cecil or return home immediately. Love—DAD."

"I think 'while murder' is beautifully expressive, and how like your father not to know that the Cecil has been pulled down. Are you going to take his advice?"

"No," said Viola. "I know it's ghoulish of me, but I must stay on to the end."

"Good. Now give your close attention to the question of Mrs Walton. Somewhere, chasing round the back of my head, is some vague, elusive memory. I'm sure I've seen her before."

Viola wrinkled her eyes in intense concentration. "How funny—I've had that idea, too. I can't decide whether I really have seen her before, or whether it is one of those illusions one gets, you know. Two sides of the brain business. I forget how the explanation goes."

"The more I try to think where I have seen her face, the less I can place it," confessed Charles. "If I don't think about it, it will probably come back."

III

"You lazy blighter," interjected Bray's voice behind him. "Haven't you stirred from where I left you?"

"I favour the static school of detection," Charles grinned. "It is no more unsuccessful than the dynamic school, and much less exhausting."

"I've just been speaking to the manager Tarr has put in," Bray said. "His horror when I told him about the history of the hotel could not have been more intense if he had been asked to take charge of a house of ill-fame. However, he is carrying on, with a look of quiet distaste on his face. Meanwhile, the hotel is slowly emptying. Miss Mumby left with her retinue of cats an hour ago. Cantrip and Winterton are already packing, and Mrs Salterton-Deeley will go as soon as she has recovered from a nervous breakdown. Nothing will move Miss Geranium, however. She is sitting in her room waiting for the final judgment of the Lord, which she asserts is near at hand."

"And Blood?"

"Blood came to me and made a clean breast of the whole thing," Bray answered. "You were right. He was the source of supply. He has closed his laboratory and is realizing all his worldly goods. I thought at first he was trying to tell me that he was going to leave the country, but it appears that he is going to fulfil his secret longing and join the Community of the Pauline Brothers at Tooting."

"He will be happy," Charles said decisively. "The habit of the Pauline Brothers is the most decorative and varied of any of the Anglo-Catholic Orders. Poor Blood," he went on seriously, "I am afraid he is a little too yielding for this wicked world. A contemplative life will give more scope to the better side of his nature than an active one."

"I am not too keen on all this scattering," the Inspector said, "but I can't very well prevent it. It's going to mean more work keeping an eye on them all. Still, Twing and Eppoliki and Mrs Walton are staying on for a little. Twing and Eppoliki are looking for somewhere to go. Twing, by the way, is abjectly afraid that I may breathe something about his little weakness in the issuing house of whom he is the honoured partner, and even Eppoliki had the grace to hope that nothing would come to the ears of his rich father in Cairo, of whom he is apparently the spoiled and extravagant darling."

The three were silent for a moment. Charles saw the Garden Hotel as a sinking ship from which the rats were already running. Its trim stucco exterior still gleamed as brightly as ever. Thanks to the loyal executorship of Tarr, the tiled doorsteps were still spotless, but the water was gushing inside, and her doom was sealed. She was a slave ship at the best, thought Charles, one of the strangest and most outrageous craft that had ever burdened the grey and dingy bosom of Kensington. Yet before, with flags flying, she took the final, irrevocable downward plunge, Charles felt determined to solve the mystery that had so far obstinately defied his searching. The chill of neglect and failure was already hovering in the corridors of the place; the servants slouched, with the consciousness of their house's doom, but he felt determined to remain until he knew what assassin had walked through to Mrs Budge's bedroom and strangled her on her bed, and what avidity of slaying had anticipated the gallows and the hangman.

Viola broke the silence. "I suppose nobody is really what they seem," she said at last. "My fellow-residents dope fiends, my hotel proprietress and her husband complete rascals and blackmailers, and even Charles, the most innocuous-looking of mortals, and transparently honest, had concealed from me the romantic fact that he was a detective for two years. Really, I shouldn't be surprised after all if Mrs Walton isn't the soft-hearted angel she looks."

"Don't get cynical," admonished Charles. "It looks bad in one so young. Nobody who can eat treacle roll with the gusto shown by Mrs Walton can be altogether bad. Certainly it absolves her from the charge of doping."

He turned to Bray. "I want to have another look at the Budges' suite," he said. "Will you come along with me? There is a certain little theory whose possibility, or rather whose impossibility, I should like to make certain of, and I want someone to help me by holding the other end of a tape measure."

Bray assented, but Viola elected to stay behind.

Charles paused outside the door, his fingers on the handle. "There's someone in here," he said.

Bray frowned. "They've no business to be," he said. "No one is supposed to go in there without my permission. There's a seal on the door which has been broken."

He listened. They could distinctly hear a rattling of drawers being opened and papers fluttered.

Silently Charles turned the handle, and then twitched the door open. A figure was bending over the bureau in the corner, sorting the papers with the energy of despair.

"Can I help you?" said Charles clearly and distinctly.

The figure wheeled round with a cry of fright.

"You!" said the detective in surprise.

It was Mrs Walton.

Mrs Walton said nothing. There was a long silence.

"Can we help you?" Charles repeated his question with a reassuring smile.

The colour slowly returned to Mrs Walton's face. She nervously clasped her fingers but spoke in a level voice. "I suppose I shouldn't really have done this, but I was looking for a private paper which Mr Budge took care of for me."

"We have been through all those papers," the detective said coldly. "If you will describe it I can tell you whether it was there."

"It was a private paper. I—I expect it has gone—been destroyed." Her voice died away unconvincingly.

Bray did not answer. He fumbled in his jacket pocket and produced an envelope. With his eyes on her face he inserted his thumb and drew out the marriage certificate which had been among the papers given by Mrs Budge into her solicitor's safe keeping.

"Was this it?" he said, unfolding it.

Impossible not to notice the horrified start that she gave, impossible not to see the skin on her temples bleach ivory, drained of its blood! But she met his eyes bravely.

"No, oh, no! I've never seen that before." With hands locked behind her, she achieved a laugh.

Bray tried an appeal. "Mrs Walton, we are only anxious to help. If we seem to pry into secrets it is with no intention of using them against whoever confides in us. Can you not be a little more frank?"

Mrs Walton inclined her head. She spoke slowly. "You are evidently suffering from some delusion. I am sorry if I was going through the bureau without permission, but I happened to remember this small private matter and hardly thought it was worth troubling you. The paper I was looking for had a sentimental interest—nothing more."

Charles stood aside and let her pass. As the door closed the two exchanged glances. "Not a very convincing liar," observed Charles. "Are we right in presuming it was her marriage certificate and that she was either Mary Church or was married under that name?"

"I suppose so," said the detective, "and now she has emerged as Mrs Walton. There are a good many possibilities here." He looked thoughtful. "I suppose I shall have to go up to Coventry to see if we can trace either of the parties mentioned from that end."

"The most obvious deduction—and therefore perhaps a dangerous one," said Charles, "is that there is something about this first marriage which would make dear old Addington—the soul of respectability—cry off if he knew. In which case we must put down some real, honest-to-goodness blackmail to the discredit of the Budges as well as dope-peddling. I wish to the Lord I could remember where I had seen her before, because I'll swear that her face is familiar."

That night Bray took the train to Coventry.

II

The little Egyptian had something of importance to say. That was evident from the way in which he had drawn Charles aside, casting a furtive monocular glance around him before speaking.

"Still no trace of the murderer, eh?" he asked.

"Lots of traces," Charles answered. "But devil a murderer."

Eppoliki grinned. "Not easy by any means. Easier sometimes trailing dope fiends than finding murderers." He gave a friendly grin.

Charles started. "And how do you know that I have any experience of trailing dope fiends?"

"Your friend Cunningham, father's pet aversion," he explained verblessly. "My father high up in narcotic trade—captain of the industry, eh?—and he have little album photographs of 'Cunningham's Chicks.' I had to learn faces by heart when I was in business. Recognize you at once, of course."

Charles laughed. "So that was it! I am afraid I scared you when I arrived."

"I knew then that Garden Hotel was ended. I admire very much neat way you murder Mrs Budge."

"Well I'm damned! Are you accusing me of polishing off the old lady as part of my professional duties? As a matter of fact, I left the Bureau years ago and I came here with no idea that it was anything but what it purported to be."

Eppoliki lifted a restraining hand. "No, no. I see later impossible you commit it. Then I say who? Now one very suspicious circumstance there is. Diagnosis is dangerous, of course, but I say 'Here symptom that point very favourably to conclusion—clear, clinical picture perhaps.'"

Eppoliki again glanced round the room apprehensively. Then he whispered in Charles's ear.

"You are absolutely certain?" Charles answered incredulously.

Eppoliki nodded. "Use it how you like. If right, then at trial you can give Eppoliki credit—failed M.B., perhaps, several times, but still notice something that prove not too bad doctor."

"Not only shall it be mentioned at the trial," Charles answered him, "but it will receive prominent treatment in the *Mercury*."

The Egyptian's white teeth flashed. "One other request—more important," he said. "If you should meet my father, professionally perhaps, keep dark about son taking narcotics. That would be very very sad to him, he thinking son becoming great professional man in London at expense of profits in drug trade."

The white teeth flashed again and Eppoliki shuffled away. That evening he left the Garden Hotel.

III

Sitting by herself in the lounge, Viola sketched idly on a pad. There was quite a lot of work for her to do—a poster for the Anthrax Collieries, a carton for an old-established brand of suet, and a cover for a newly established fashion paper, but she could not concentrate on any of these things. Her thoughts insistently returned to what the world knew as the Garden Hotel Mystery.

Viola thought best with a pencil in her hand, and the paper before her rapidly darkened with scribbling. Miss Mumby's face loomed with a sinister emphasis out of the façade of the hotel, and an elvish Budge dangled helplessly from a telephone receiver. Free association lent her pencil inspiration, and Mrs Walton's classic profile emerged from a sea of trouble. Viola's flying pencil stopped, then started again. This time it was a clown's pointed hat, and free association ended when she had to make an intellectual decision as to the number and position of the pom-poms on it.

"Now why a clown's hat?" her brain demanded wonderingly. Something in the mist clicked, and she was five years back, at the circus at Olympia. There was the light, the noise and the dust and trampling of the ring. In her recollection a clown or two were lounging on the barrier, but her thought, the thoughts of the multitude which packed the stands, magnified by memory, were concentrated upwards. There in the brilliance of arc-lights a slip of a girl darted like a rosy-breasted bird through a gossamer web of wires. The trapeze described its glittering arc, and she swung from it, one wrist carelessly linking it to the taut spring of her body. Then she fell, like a rose-petal, through sheer space. Viola heard again that sigh of fear as she dropped, mellowing into relief as her partner below, at the zenith of his trapeze's swing, stretched outwards, wrists extended and, hanging only by the friction of his ankles, linked hands with her as she passed.

Mary Church, the "Human Swallow," was the star turn at the circus that year, and Viola had spent hours endeavouring to fix on paper those matchless curves of the flying, straining human body, and when, night after night, the Human Swallow had come near the seat where Viola sat to take her call, Viola had been able to pin her lovely features to the paper. And definitely—oh, indisputably—those features were the features of Mrs Walton.

"Can I see—or are you one of those artists who hate to have their work viewed in its preliminary rawness?" It was Miss Sanctuary's voice, and Viola made room for her on the sofa on which she was sitting.

"It isn't work," she said. "Just idling. But it is idling that has brought me some reward. I have stumbled on a discovery which may help to solve our mystery."

The grey-haired woman shuddered. "How I regret the part I played in that. Inspector Bray was extraordinarily nice about it, possibly because, as his manner plainly showed, he thought I wasn't in full possession of my wits. I acted madly on the spur of the moment, and, you see, my action involved the man I wanted to help in speedier ruin than if I had let things take their course. It makes one a fatalist, but even the comforting reflection of Kismet cannot prevent one feeling some of the guilt."

"Nonsense," said Viola reassuringly. "Yours was a kindly action, and, if what the Inspector says is true, the man was doomed by whoever killed him from the moment of his arrest."

"Thank you," smiled Miss Sanctuary. "It has taught me never to interfere again." She seemed to shake the memory from her, and went on in a more normal voice. "Tell me, what is this discovery of yours?"

"I'll show you," said Viola mysteriously. She tore the top sheet off the pad. Her pencil travelled deftly, guided by the remembering brain. A thistle-down figure, a miracle of suppleness, lay arched across the bar of a trapeze, the body foreshortened to exaggerate the feline tension of the limbs. The figure looked out of the paper, and the face was the face of the Human Swallow, of Mrs Walton.

Miss Sanctuary stared at it. "Good heavens, child," she said at last, blank astonishment in her face, "what put this into your head?"

"That's a circus girl I saw four or five years ago. She was *the* turn at Olympia, and I remember her well because I sketched her at the time. She is Mrs Walton. I am as certain of that as I am certain that I'm Viola Merritt."

"Amazing," murmured Miss Sanctuary, "amazing! You've told Bray, I suppose?"

"I think I shall tell Charles and together we'll see if we can't get a beat on Bray," answered Viola. "It'll be much more fun to do it unprofessionally, and he will get tremendous *kudos* if this thing has any bearing on the case."

"What makes you think it has?" asked the old lady.

"I heard Bray telling Charles that there was something mysterious about Mrs Walton, and that if they could only get on to that, he felt sure they might come across the loose thread that would bring them to the solution. I don't think Mrs Walton is personally implicated—I'm sure she isn't—but they believe she has the key of the mystery, and she's so very secretive."

Miss Sanctuary smiled at her eagerness, the eternal appetite for the hunt, for the hue and cry, which is an instinct as old as humanity.

"Why not investigate it yourself? Think how surprised Mr Venables would be if you had done a little detective work on your own and got ahead of him."

Viola's eyes brightened. "I say, that would be rather fun," she exclaimed. "Where should one start, now?"

"There is a very old friend of mine, Mrs Mortimer, who knows almost all there is to know about circuses. She followed one in a caravan for five years, and I think she has friends in every circus in Europe. You may know her book *White Sand*. No? Well, it was a little too true to circus life, I think, to be a best-seller, but she will be able to tell you more about the Human Swallow than anyone else in England."

Miss Sanctuary smiled ironically. "You mustn't blame me if you are disappointed. Life isn't quite what we expect, and the more mysterious a thing looks, the more prosaic it is as a rule in essence. It is the ordinary happenings that can have the most sinister causes. You may feel rather sorry you troubled to track down Mrs Walton's secret."

She fished in her large grey bag and produced a tiny pencil and a scrap of paper. "Here you are," she said, writing "*Mrs Mortimer, Pentecost, Lima Road, Tooting.*"

Meanwhile Bray followed a scent five years old in Coventry registry office, hotel and theatre... Endless questions... the vagueness of the human mind... But the link between Mary Church and Mrs Walton shaped itself and strengthened.

I V

"Have you a photograph of yourself, Mrs Walton?" said Charles. "All right, Addington, don't glare. I only want it to adorn one of those charming little paragraphs I write, you know. Now that our little mystery is dying away, I am returning to the gossip column."

Addington's blue eyes blazed. "For God's sake don't associate her with this wretched business here. I've tried to persuade her to move, but she insists that it is not worth while with so short a time to go to the wedding."

"That's all right," answered the journalist. "I'll be admirably discreet. By the way, if it isn't impertinent, and don't answer it if it is, where did you meet?"

Two pairs of eyes met. Two faces softened with memories shared and treasured. "On a cruise," Mrs Walton said. "The West Indies. Those stars! I sometimes think I must have imagined them."

"And that moon! I loved you from the first moment you came into the dining-room, with your dreamy stare round."

"Short-sightedness, dear," smiled the other.

"…and, by Jove, weren't you standoffish? At the end of the voyage I came to the conclusion you thoroughly disliked me."

"Well, you see it was just after losing my husband." Her face clouded. "You know… I've told you… that wasn't a success, and I felt that I wanted to be by myself, and never, never be dependent on anyone again. I said to myself that never would I put myself in a position where my privacy and my loneliness would be at the mercy of anyone. And no sooner had I made this resolution than I found myself wanting to spend my time with a man I'd never seen before until I walked into the ship's dining-room and saw you at the Captain's table."

"So you did see me, in spite of your short-sightedness!" laughed Addington. "And then after that cruise we never saw each other for two years until I saw you walking down Bond Street, and you remembered me, and we went to Ranelagh—"

"And just as you were saying good-bye, you asked me to marry you!"

"Shall I slink off or crawl away on all fours?" Charles asked himself. This was unbearable. "I must pop off now," he mumbled. "About that photo?"

"Oh, I've got two," said Addington. He fished in his wallet. "I think we can spare you one. Here you are!"

Addington's eyes lingered as he gazed at it before handing it over.

It was a good photograph—that is to say, it was a snapshot, and had not been touched up into a professionally misty caricature. Mrs Walton's looks survived even ordeal by camera.

"Anyway," he consoled himself, "she has a perfect alibi for the murder, and whatever mud I stir up, it won't be that." He made the mental reservation to suppress any information he came upon, if he so thought good.

Charles, too, had that feeling that there was something familiar in Mrs Walton's face. She obviously did not know him, and he assumed that she had been at some time in the public eye. If that were so, then somewhere in the *Mercury* office should be someone who could put his finger on time, place, and name.

Every big newspaper office is a repository of forgotten secrets, or secrets that have never come to life. If you have been in the thick of every *cause célèbre*, if you have streaked like a hound on the faintest scent of a "story," if you have sat through long police-court proceedings of which the greater part could not be published, if you have read the "private and confidential" letters to the editor giving the well-authenticated intimate information which the law of libel and public policy will not let you publish, if the principal actor in many a sorry drama has tried to justify his action to you with a final "But of course this is not for publication, old boy," and if you have in addition a brain whose professional pride it is to store this information away for reference when necessary—then you would realize why Charles took the faded but truthful snapshot to the offices of his paper.

He started with the art editor, Perry, whose incredible immaculacy was proverbial in Fleet Street. Perhaps the only man in England who habitually made up the picture page in a frock-coat, a white slip, spats, and a carnation, Perry could turn suddenly from a lounging fashion-plate to a raging, tearing piece of energy, who dispatched aeroplanes, racing cars, and on one historic occasion three teams of Eskimo dogs, to bring back the precious plates.

"Congratulations, Charles," he remarked, eyeing the photograph professionally. "I am afraid it will not reproduce very well."

"Who is she?" asked Charles.

Perry looked surprised. "Good heavens, did you forget to ask her name? How awkward!"

"Joking apart," said Charles wearily, "will you bring your brains to bear upon the problem of identifying this lady? Has she ever been through your hands—in the negative, I mean?"

Perry thought for five minutes. "I have a vague recollection I've seen something like it on the box of chocolates I bought my wife yesterday, that's all. Sorry."

Next in order of likelihood was the librarian. Isaac Hubbard had a system of filing press cuttings so ingenious and with cross reference so elaborate that it was believed that he could find anything that had appeared in the British Press for fifty years past in fifty seconds. His files were so rich in material that the breath had hardly left a distinguished subject's body before the *Mercury*'s evening newspaper was on the streets with a fuller account of his life than any of its rivals. The only fault of the system was that it was so ingenious, it was believed that no one but Hubbard could ever grasp its complexities. The matter had never been put to the test, however, for Hubbard, a long-armed hunchback, with huge tortoiseshell spectacles and a squeaky voice, appeared to live permanently in the library, without taking a holiday from year's end to year's end. Legend said that in gloom and silence he expiated the dreadful memory of the one mistake of his life, twenty-five years ago, when a man, eminent in that day, named Arthur Thurston, had died and Hubbard had given the reporter who was due to write his obituary, the folder of his still-living namesake.

Hubbard scrutinized the snapshot in silence. "A very lovely lady," he said at last, "but I do not know her face. I should say almost for certain she hasn't appeared in our paper." Seeing Charles's disappointment, he went on: "Of course I'm not answerable for the advertisement columns, and if it were an actress or a film star it is just possible—why not see Mr Hardy?"

Hardy, the advertisement manager, had only two ambitions in life. One was to see the total number of single column inches of display advertising appearing in the *Mercury* in a year exceed that of its rival, and the other was to be mistaken for Lord Bensdale by a friend of that peer. So far, at that date, they were only five thousand inches behind their rival's figures, and only two days before at a city banquet a cousin of Lord Bensdale had stared incredulously at Hardy, and was apparently on the verge of speaking to him. As a result, Hardy was in a mellow mood when Charles spoke to him.

"Do I know it? Why, don't I see that face every time I go into the reps' room? Come with me!"

The reps burst into activity as Hardy entered. He led Charles up to a sheet of brown paper on which were pasted a whole collection of pretty ladies who had appeared in the advertising columns of the *Mercury*. His forefinger stabbed the centre one. With arms extended, form displayed with all the cold emphasis of the camera, was, so the headline in battering black "sans" informed the reader, the "Human Swallow, twice nightly." Absorbed in her feat, unconscious of the camera, the "Human Swallow" looked out of the paper. The face was that of Mrs Walton.

"A circus turn!" exclaimed Charles.

Hardy laughed. "Did you think you had got off with a duchess?"

Charles ignored the remark. "Now where could I get hold of more information about that turn? I see it is over five years since it was advertised in the *Mercury*."

Hardy thought a moment. "I don't think you can do better than go to Menzies. He is press agent for half the leading circus people, and he knows all the circus families and their connections—and you could number the people who can do that on one hand. He is probably press agent to the Human Swallow." Hardy scribbled an address on the back of his card.

V

Charles had been astonished at his discovery of the beautiful Mrs Walton's lurid past. What was she doing now, apparently moderately well off, and about to be married to a man very definitely belonging to society? What strange secrets were buried in that past; and what was the import of this marriage certificate for it to be an instrument of blackmail in the hands of the Budges?

Charles's speculation was cut short by the arrival of a note from Viola.

"DEAR OLD THING," she wrote, "the post is so infernally efficient, you will probably get this in Fleet Street almost at once. Prepare yourself for a shock. I am on the track of big things.

"Mrs Walton has a lurid past! Quite by accident I suddenly remembered where I had seen her face—she was a circus turn at Olympia five years ago. There!

"I confided in Miss Sanctuary, and she has given me the name of a woman friend of hers who knows all about circuses. She lives in Tooting, of all places, and in a house called Pentecost!

"I'm going along there now to discover what I can, but I've been simply boiling over with excitement, and felt I must tell you what had happened! I hope to have some really interesting news when I have seen Mrs Mortimer, but don't be surprised if my investigations take me to China or Peru or somewhere. We detectives, you know.

"Ever thine,

"VIOLA."

Charles smiled ruefully. If anything, Viola was ahead of him in the investigations. What would Xavier have said?

"Never make use of a woman for criminal detection," he used to caution his operatives. "They are incapable of the sheerly logical processes—devoid of emotional prejudice—which are the instruments of the investigator's art!"

"I suppose I had better back my press agent against Miss Sanctuary's woman friend!" Charles concluded. "I hope to goodness Viola pumps her properly."

Menzies lived in an extraordinary block of offices off the Charing Cross Road. A dirty, blistered door confronted one, plastered with the tarnished brass plates of a score of dubious enterprises. There was no knocker or bell, but violent hammering with his umbrella on a susceptible panel eventually brought a suspicious and frowsty "char" to the door. An ancient and carpetless staircase seemed to wind endlessly up without reaching any offices until eventually it fulfilled its proper function with a rush and one found one's head emerging on a level with the floor of an ante-room. As one rose, piles of playbills and autographed photographs of all sizes were visible, whose age could be approximately dated by the thickness of the dust upon them. Waves of steak and onions, mingled with the trilling of a piano, drifted from the apparently residential quarters upstairs. The char flung open a door at the end of the ante-room and discovered Menzies in his shirtsleeves gloomily concentrated over a current *Punch*. Tall, pale, with large horn-rimmed glasses and a waxen complexion, Menzies bore about him more of the atmosphere of æsthetics than of ballyhoo. But he was notoriously efficient at his job.

Hardy's introduction was good enough for him. "The Human Swallow?" he said. "That's a curious thing. Only the other day I was wondering what had become of little Mary Church—that was her name before she married an Italian juggler called Sarto."

"Tell me anything you can about her, will you?" asked Charles. "What was she doing in the circus business, for instance?"

"Good heavens, man!" answered Menzies reprovingly, "you don't need to ask what a Church is doing in the circus business— they've been in it for ages. This particular branch of the family have been managers of a prosperous little travelling circus for at least five generations. I dimly remember the grandfather—a fine-looking man and remarkably well educated. He married the daughter of a local bigwig, Sir John Fitzhatter, at Market Hatterton—a runaway match it was and created a terrible scandal in those days, so that Church's Circus never visited Market Hatterton again. The girl was completely ostracized by the family, but I believe she was quite happy.

"There was no son, but one daughter. She used to give acrobatic turns—trapeze work and so on—but when her father died she took over the management of the circus and did it remarkably well. She was a brilliant woman, who would have succeeded in almost any line, I think. She had been in expensive schools, and talked and behaved like a lady, but the circus was in her blood and she married Ferdinand Church, a distant cousin of hers and a very decent sort, so that the show still remained Church's Circus.

"They also had no son—only a daughter—and that was your Human Swallow. I always maintained that she was wasted on those acrobatic turns, although admittedly she had a perfect body. But she was beautiful, really beautiful, and she should have gone on the stage. But the father wouldn't hear of it—didn't consider it respectable—and that ended it.

"Then came the tragedy. There was an Italian juggler named Giovanni Sarto, brilliant at his job and a pleasant enough fellow personally, I thought, with that classic curly handsomeness that you see in some Italians. Mary lost her head with the completeness of the spoiled only child who had been rather shielded from that sort of thing all her life, and they were married in a Coventry registry office. Sarto wouldn't stay with the Church Circus; he thought it was too small for either of them, and as a businessman I agreed with him. They went to America."

Menzies paused. His pale face clouded with the memory of an ancient wrong. Charles divined that even to the indurated press agent, the Human Swallow had been something more than a mere client.

"No one knows what exactly took place on that American tour. But she came back with the eyes of a ghost, of somebody dead who would never come to life again. Sarto drank, apparently, and that was the least of his failings. Some people have a genius for cruelty; they make an art of it. There was none of the crudity of wife-beating about Sarto, I gathered. Instead, he made her suffer every imaginable humiliation—if possible publicly—and shocked every sensitive nerve in her mind into horror. Yet so strong was his mental ascendancy over her that it was not until one day when he fell off the ladder on which he was juggling and was in bed for three days, that she could key herself up to revolt and run back home.

"Soon after that this branch of the Churches disappeared from circus life. The father died—they said the shock killed him, but he was getting on and probably the doctor's verdict of pneumonia was nearer the truth. Mrs Church suddenly had plenty of money, and my theory is that the grandson of the original Fitzhatter—this grandson was a charming fellow who had died not long before—had ended the family feud and left some of his money to Mrs Church—his cousin. Anyway, she never said anything, and I wasn't sufficiently curious to go to Somerset House and find out for certain. The last thing I remember about them was seeing Mrs Church in my office, sitting where you are sitting now. She had been by way of being a good friend of mine, and although her visit was ostensibly to pay me for the press publicity I had done in connection with the sale of the circus animals and properties, I think it was really to say good-bye. 'My daughter's an invalid, Menzies,' she said to me, 'not physically, but mentally. I've got to nurse her back to health, and I've got to cut away from all the old associations. We shall have to storm a new world together. I feel terribly responsible for the tragedy—I, who pride myself on my perception, not to see the sort of poisonous reptile Sarto was! Well, I'm going to devote the rest of my life to restoring her to health and happiness. It's too late to do anything with Sarto now—I can't even trace him in America—but, by heavens, if any other man tries to wreck my daughter's happiness again—' Mrs Church was a mild-mannered, soft-spoken woman—one of those charming old ladies that beam on everyone—but when she said that I thought that not for a million pounds would I like to be in the shoes of Sarto, or of any other man who was responsible for that look appearing in Mary's eyes again."

Menzies flicked the ash off the end of his cigar. "Since then I've never heard another word from them, or about them. I don't know whether Mrs Church ever nursed poor Mary Sarto back to a state where she looked at a thing as if it existed, or at a person without cringing. But she managed to disappear. As a pressman, I reckon to run across most people, but I've never run across either of them. Probably, though, they're here in London—in one of London's many worlds which are as separate as planets—the West End fashionable world, or the Jermyn Street naughty world, or the Kensington respectable world, or the suburban bourgeois world, or the Bloomsbury intellectual world. Anyway, they're gone, and there's an end of it. How the years flee, my Posthumus. Have a drink?"

"Thanks," said Charles. "I haven't quite finished troubling you. Here's the last straw. Have you a photograph of Sarto?"

"I'll see if I can dig one up," he answered.

Like many people whose office is apparently littered with hopelessly confounded and scattered rubbish, he really had a secret but highly effective filing system which enabled him to find what he wanted in a short time, at the price of somewhat dusty fingers. After a few minutes' rummaging he pulled out a wooden tray marked "Church's Circus," and ran through the contents.

"Here you are," he said at last. "A photograph of the wedding-party, with Mary Church and Sarto, fond mother and father, and various circus friends."

Charles glanced at it. His casual regard stiffened to concentration. He gazed open-mouthed at the photograph. Menzies saw his face whiten and the jaw muscles grow tense.

"Is anything wrong?" he asked, peering at the photo.

"There is," answered Charles, galvanized into an embodiment of action. "For God's sake don't ask any questions, but do what I tell you." His voice was shaking. "It is a matter of life and death."

Charles spoke slowly and distinctly. "Phone up Inspector Bray at Scotland Yard—say you are speaking for me—and tell him to call with the flying squad tender at this address. Tell him not to fail me—tell him I've found the murderer."

Menzies stared. He still stared as Charles whirled out of the room, and he continued staring as he heard his clatter down the ancient stairs die away. Then he picked up the phone and asked for Scotland Yard.

As he spoke, there was a shout in the street outside. It was from the indignant owner of a Grand Prix Mercedes, who had arrived in time to see its tail disappear as it skidded round the corner in Charles's capable hands. A little later he heard a subdued whine as Charles cut in the supercharger half-way up Charing Cross Road.

The indignant owner was put through to Scotland Yard about three minutes after Menzies had been connected to Bray.

Chapter Sixteen

THE MURDERER IS CORNERED

"Pentecost" was a rambling old house that looked as if it had been the centre of a large estate in the days when Tooting was "in the country." Now the tide of villadom had surged around and over its former splendours, but had still left it enough garden and grounds to make it one of the outstanding houses of the suburb.

Viola wandered up a path flanked by dusty shrubs. There were weeds everywhere. Amateur of the circus though she may have been, Mrs Mortimer was no garden lover. A "To Let" board slouched oafishly in the front—evidently the depression of "Pentecost" had been too much even for Mrs Mortimer. A disquieting thought struck Viola. "I hope she hasn't moved since Miss Sanctuary heard from her last."

A pull at the old-fashioned bell woke echoes in the house. She heard someone walk briskly up from the basement. The door opened, and in the semi-shadow stood an old woman with a lace mantilla which shadowed her face. She was leaning on a stick.

"Can I see Mrs Mortimer?" asked Viola.

"I'm Mrs Mortimer," answered the old lady, peering at her inquiringly from the darkness.

"I was sent to you by Miss Sanctuary. You see, I wanted to trace someone in the circus world, and she said you would be able to help me."

"I expect I can," answered the other in her low, curiously gruff voice, "if anyone can. Come in." The door was closed and the corridor was in darkness. "Straight ahead," said the old lady, and put her hand on Viola's shoulder to guide her.

Suddenly the frail hand stiffened to a grip of steel. It met its fellow round Viola's throat, and the cry she uttered changed into a gurgling. Intense lights danced on the darkness before Viola's eyes; and then she became unconscious...

I I

For a time phantasma merged with characters of ordinary life in the weird dreams that hurried through her mind. When she came into full consciousness she saw a bare grey room with the dust of years upon it. She felt bare boards under her, and her legs were devoid of feeling. They were bound. Her breath came slowly and with difficulty, for she was gagged. She was alone for a time; then the door opened, and the old woman came in. Instinctively, bound as she was, she shrunk away, and then the old woman stepped into the light of the window. The black lace that had shadowed her face was thrown back and the light fell full upon it. It was Miss Sanctuary.

Miss Sanctuary saw recognition blaze in the girl's eye. She came and sat down beside her on a wooden box, looking down calmly and indifferently at the bound girl.

"Yes, it is I," she said wearily. "I murdered the Budges. They blackmailed my daughter. They never guessed that the demure little lady who insisted on staying at the hotel was Mrs Walton's mother. But the police would have found out if you had told them of your discovery, and so I sent you here. The house agent thought I was a very likely purchaser when I asked for the key." Miss Sanctuary laughed mirthlessly, and looked at the girl, her lips pursed. "I brought you here to kill you, of course." She stated the fact calmly, without malice or fury.

Viola, frightened though she was, and still shaky from the physical effects of the assault, could yet fathom the deep-seated purpose of this woman.

"I have come into this room twice," stated Miss Sanctuary, "with the intention of strangling you while you were unconscious, yet I haven't been able to do it." Her tone was faintly surprised. "These hands"—her voice quivered as she looked down at them—"somehow wouldn't obey the orders of the brain. You are not like the Budges, I suppose. Anyway, I simply cannot do it."

There was neither remorse nor the petty fear of guilt in her level tone. Her purpose, which had enabled her to contemplate capital crime with equanimity, may have verged on mania, may have been mania, but she couldn't murder this girl, even for the sake of her daughter, and she was puzzled.

"Will you promise not to shout if I remove your gag?" she said at last.

Viola nodded her head, and with deft fingers Miss Sanctuary removed the cramping bandage. Their eyes met—would-be murderer and unwilling victim.

"I might let you go free," said Miss Sanctuary after a while, "if you promised on your solemn word of honour not to breathe a syllable of your discovery of my daughter's identity, or of what has taken place to-day, or of anything that might lead to the discovery of my daughter's identity."

"Why are you so anxious to keep it secret?" asked Viola.

"It is the price of my daughter's happiness," affirmed the other. "Five years ago my daughter was married. The man was a scoundrel. It is impossible to describe the unhappiness he brought into my daughter's life; and I thought for a time she would never really and truly smile again. It was just as if something had snapped in her mind, and as if she could never see any goodness or kindness in humanity again. Then she went for a cruise to the West Indies, and when she came back it was just as if she had come back to life again. It wasn't so much that she was happier. It was more that her heart had been turned to ice before and now it had melted and she could cry—and therefore laugh as well.

"It was not till a year ago that I found out the reason for this change. It was a man she had met on the boat and whom she met again—St Clair Addington. He loves her, in his way, and he is a gentleman, and she is violently and absolutely in love with him—drinks up his consideration and his little kindnesses as a flower drinks up rain."

Miss Sanctuary paused, and when she spoke again her voice was icy with a cold distaste. "Then she fell into the hands of those abominable Budges! As if she had not had enough misfortune, she came to that hotel without realizing its true character, and was taken in as a guest whose innocence would cover up their suspicious activities. One day Budge recognized her and ferreted out the truth. When he saw her engagement to Addington he saw his opportunity. One word to Addington, the soul of respectability, would be enough—bigamy!"

Miss Sanctuary laughed mirthlessly. "My daughter and I had long put Sarto out of our minds—to us he was dead and she was a widow. But in the eyes of the law—bigamy! So he bled her steadily, and anxiety began to give that dead look to her eyes that she had when she ran away from Sarto. The past was over-taking her again." Miss Sanctuary sat bolt upright, looking beyond the horizon, her eyes pools of fire. "I decided to put an end to it. As a harmless old spinster I came and stayed at the hotel."

The fires of fury died away in her cold eyes. "Both knew me before they died. I was judge and jury and executioner."

Even in that room and those surroundings, Viola found it difficult to grasp the suddenness of the transition from Miss Sanctuary, the kindly old maid, to the avenging Nemesis who sat beside her and spoke calmly of murder and strangulation. She shuddered as she realized that twice the woman had been in the room while she lay unconscious, and eyed her throat with speculative eyes, and then had drawn back because she was not fundamentally a killer, but a harassed mother with the atavistic fixity of purpose of a less squeamish age.

"If you release me," said Viola at last, as steadily as she could, "I will give you my solemn word of honour not to give away the slightest hint of your secret to anyone."

"I am compounding a felony," she thought to herself, "and promises made under duress are not legally binding, but I shall have to make the promise and I shall have to keep it. I wonder if the murderer will ever be discovered?"

Miss Sanctuary was looking at her as if to fathom her most secret thoughts. The results of her scrutiny seemed to satisfy her. "Very well."

Suddenly Viola recollected her letter to Charles. "Good heavens!" she said. "Before I came here I wrote to Charles!"

Miss Sanctuary's eyes glittered. "You told him?" she said.

III

Her question was answered. With a crash that seemed to shock the silence of the house the window was shattered and a man leaped into the room, his face shielded with a macintosh.

"Venables!" exclaimed Miss Sanctuary, rising to her feet.

Charles did not waste time in formalities. He sprang on Miss Sanctuary and seized her by the wrist. With a strength incredible in anyone of her age she struggled with him, but he had the advantage of surprise and skill. In a few minutes she was sitting on the box with her hands and feet more neatly trussed than Viola's.

Charles untied the rope round Viola's wrists and ankles, and chafed them. "Thank God you are all right! I thought I should be too late. I never guessed who she was till I saw her photograph in Menzies' room."

He helped Viola to her feet. She pressed her hand to her forehead. She felt uncommonly shaky now that the ordeal was over. She laughed weakly.

"When it came to the pinch she found that she couldn't do me in," Viola said. "So we were just evolving a gentleman's agreement, or rather a lady's agreement, whereby I should promise to keep things dark and in return I should be released."

"Yes, it was rather foolish of me," said Miss Sanctuary briskly. "Yet when it came to the pinch I found I wasn't as ruthless as I thought!"

Charles rubbed his chin thoughtfully. "It sounds rather banal to thank you," he said. "It certainly complicates matters. Heavens, what's that?"

"That" was the bell, clanging imperiously in the basement. "Oh, Lord! Of course," Charles went on, "it's Bray."

It was Bray, with four constables spoiling for the fray. Bray metaphorically rubbed his eyes at the tableau—Charles with blood dripping from a cut in his hand, Miss Sanctuary sitting bound hand and foot on a wooden box, and Viola leaning shakily against the wall.

"What's all this?"

Miss Sanctuary spoke. Her voice was clear and unemotional. "I wilfully murdered Mrs Budge and Mr Budge," she said. "I must categorically refuse to make any other statement, however, until I have had legal advice."

"You!" exclaimed Bray incredulously. He turned to Charles. "What *is* the meaning of all this?" he asked.

"It looks like being a very involved story," answered Charles. "As Miss Sanctuary mentioned just now, she was responsible for both murders." He looked at Bray significantly. "I think at this stage, Viola and I had better have a further talk with Miss Sanctuary alone."

It was with the greatest reluctance that Bray withdrew. Charles saw a policeman take up his station outside the window. Then he turned to Miss Sanctuary. "Well, what shall we do?" he said.

"I feel that my action was thoroughly justified in both cases," answered Miss Sanctuary calmly, "but one never knows. Perhaps I should be happier if I paid the penalty. At any rate my conscience would be tidier. I am getting an old woman anyway, and there is not much left of life for me. I don't think I shall like being hanged by the neck till dead, but I shall prefer it to being respited and dying in prison." She paused, then she continued earnestly: "Mr Venables, the one thing that must not happen is for this to taint my daughter's happiness. The guilty life for the taken life is the law's demand. I am ready to satisfy it. But must my daughter, innocent even of the knowledge of my part in this affair, pay also with the wreckage of her happiness when her past is dragged through the mire of a big murder trial? Miss Sanctuary committed the crime. Cannot Miss Sanctuary pay for it?"

Charles shook his head. "I do not see how the matter could be hushed up. It is impossible to keep these things out of the cruel probing of the prosecution, even if you refuse to make any defence."

Miss Sanctuary shook her head. "There is something," she said firmly, "that would silence them, something

'that shackles accident, and bolts up change.'

I have often thought of this eventuality, and prepared for it. You will find my bag on the mantelshelf in the kitchen."

Bray, pacing impatiently up and down the corridor, looked up anxiously when Charles came out.

Charles did not fence. "Look here, Bray," he said, "this case is incredibly complicated. 'Miss Sanctuary' is Mrs Church—Mrs Walton's mother. I can get a full and complete confession from her now—on one condition, and that is that her daughter is not involved in the subsequent trial."

"But that's impossible, Charles!" protested the detective. "You must realize that yourself surely. How can the vital matter of motive be hushed up?"

"Let me put it another way," Charles said wearily. "If it is possible for you to make use of her confession and clear up the case without involving the daughter, will you do so?"

"It is a big 'if,'" replied Bray. "So big an 'if' that I haven't much hesitation in assenting."

"Right," answered Charles. He looked at Bray keenly. "I shall hold you to that, you know."

Bray went in with Charles. Miss Sanctuary fished in her bag and produced a pad and little gold fountain-pen. She wrote steadily for a few minutes, seated on the wooden box, the pad on her knee. Not a sound broke the silence but the scratching of her pen and the heavy breathing of a constable in the corner of the room.

"Here you are," she said at last.

"Being now in sound mind and body," the statement ran, "but desirous of the truth being on record, I confess that I murdered George Budge and the woman known as his wife. This statement is made of my own free will and without prompting.

"(Signed) LAURA CHURCH *alias* SANCTUARY."

IV

"I should like to write a message for my daughter, if I may?" asked Miss Sanctuary.

"Very well," the detective replied shortly. "I can give you ten minutes." He walked to the window and stared out of it.

Her message was little longer than her confession. The scratching of her pen had barely ceased when there was a faint choking sound, followed by the hurried intake of breath. Bray wheeled sharply and sprang to her side. The death agony that supervenes on the administration of prussic acid is, however, brief. When Bray reached her, Laura Church was beyond mortal aid, beyond the reach of mortal voice.

"Damn it, Charles!" said Bray angrily. "You knew about this."

"It was a private bargain between us," answered Charles.

> "Bravest at the last,
> She levelled at our purposes."

The pad on which she had been writing lay on the floor. Charles tore off the page and thrust it into his pocket.

"I will deliver this message myself," he said finally.

V

The Commissioner had placed Charles in the chair of honour, a leather armchair of royal ease. Bray shared in his glory, and sat bolt upright in a chair very nearly as luxurious. The Commissioner passed round the cigars.

"So one of Cunningham's Chicks has got ahead of us! Well, between these four walls I don't mind admitting it is not the first time."

Charles laughed. "Got ahead isn't a fair expression for either party," he protested. "By sheer luck I stumbled on the missing link needed in the chain built up by Bray. Directly I discovered that, mere suspicion became provable certainty."

"And the missing link was?"

"A photograph of 'Miss Sanctuary' and her daughter and son-in-law." Charles explained his visit to Menzies. "When I saw that, the nightmare hypothesis I had built up with Miss Sanctuary as the murderer became the only possible explanation."

"Let us begin at the beginning then," said the Commissioner wearily. "How on earth could Miss Sanctuary have committed the crime?"

"Easily," answered Charles. "I saw that from the start. She first garrottes the unsuspecting woman—an easy job with a thin piece of cord. She then ties the corpse under the big old-fashioned bed, between the spring mattress and the loose sacking. An excellent hiding-place which would never be discovered except in a proper search of the room by an expert—and all she wished to do was to gain a few minutes.

"All one needs to do—I experimented with the idea myself—is to tie the wrists and ankles to the corners of the bed and then tie the sacking underneath. There is a natural recess which makes it a perfect hiding-place."

"But the man who attacked her?" asked Bray. "Who was he?"

Charles laughed. "That, of course, was a touch of genius—a perfect alibi. I'll show you how it's done—as a matter of fact it's a little parlour trick which I used to do myself at school."

Charles got up and went outside. A moment later the door opened, and Charles's head, and the right side of his body was visible. Suddenly a gloved hand reached past the edge of the door and fastened round his neck. His expression changed from one of vacuous amiability to terror. He gurgled, but the remorseless hand, apparently exerting a giant's strength, dragged him back out of sight, and the door closed. It opened again instantly, and Charles, wreathed in smiles, a glove on one hand, appeared again to take his bow.

"Ridiculous! Childish! Absurd!" he said. "Yet see how it succeeds if properly done."

The Commissioner laughed. "I should certainly have been prepared to swear that you had been brutally assaulted in the heart of Scotland Yard. And, of course, in the circumstances in which Nurse Evans saw it, she would be bound to be deceived. Well, really! To think that we were taken in by a puerile practical joke."

Bray's ears were red with mortification, and the Commissioner stole a sly glance at him and winked at Charles.

"So far, so good," he said. "Proceed."

"The door was slammed and locked in the nurse's face, and Miss Sanctuary crept into the wardrobe with the rope she had concealed in her clothes together with a set of long-nosed pliers. She locked herself in by turning the key from the inside with the pliers—I saw the marks on the key—"

"An old dodge," commented the Commissioner, "but one expects it from burglars, not from elderly spinsters."

"Then she tied herself up neatly with the rope. It was no amateurish job, but in her circus days Laura Church could give an escape turn with chains, ropes, or strait-jacket which, even if it wasn't up to the highest professional standard, was enough to puzzle anyone but an expert, and of course by the time the police arrived we had untied her."

A gleam of amusement at last visited Bray's face. "I must tell Noakes that while he was fiddling about in the bedroom the body was there all the time!" he murmured.

"When the police had left the room she rapidly untied the body, dragged it out on to the verandah and toppled it into the next one, which, you will remember, gave her access to Budge's bedroom. I can vouch for it that she was strong, even if it is twenty-five years since she swung on a trapeze, and she had no difficulty in dealing with Mrs Budge's corpse, and packing it in the laundry basket in Budge's room.

"By that time she believed that the main part of her task was over. She went back to the bed and later on walked back to her bedroom, without the shadow of a stain of suspicion upon her.

"Her intention had been to incriminate Budge when the body was found in his room. She would then start to recollect some detail of her assault which would confirm the police's suspicion that he was the murderer. In this way both the Budges would be wiped out. She started by telling one picturesque detail next day.

"Unfortunately Budge found the body before the police, and lost no time in moving it into Blood's room. The trail was by this time hopelessly confused, but Budge only escaped arrest by his presence of mind. His acute brain searched for a possible enemy, and fixed on Mrs Walton. But Mrs Walton had an incontestable alibi. Therefore he concluded it must be some relative of the injured girl.

"He decided that if he were arrested he would make a clean breast of the whole affair and get the police to investigate the antecedents of his victim to find out whether one of the relatives was in the neighbourhood. Meanwhile he carried a revolver and locked the door at night. At last, in desperation, he went to Miss Sanctuary, the one person in the hotel with the kindness and ripe experience one looks for in a confidante, and confided his problem. Some family has a grudge against him; perhaps, he admitted cautiously, they had some grounds for it. At this point Miss Sanctuary must have smiled ironically to herself. Should he put the whole matter in the police's hands there and then, or should he wait till he was arrested? Miss

Sanctuary, needless to say, strongly advised him to wait till he was arrested. This consorted with his own views and he agreed.

"Had he confided in the police or in myself he would be alive at this day. A really searching inquiry would inevitably have traced out the relationship between Mrs Walton and Miss Sanctuary. But Nemesis, as irrevocably as in a Greek play, was drawing him on to his doom. He confided his fears to his wife's executioner.

"Next morning Miss Sanctuary was told that Budge was to be arrested. Unless her crime was to be in vain, it was necessary for her to act swiftly. She went to her room and wrote that note which would bring Budge to the toolshed and which, even if the police found it in spite of her injunction to him to burn it, would not incriminate her. There, in the toolshed, she met him. The words of gratitude on his lips were choked by her sudden revelation that she was Mrs Walton's mother. Then, before he could cry out, before perhaps the full realization of what she was saying had come to him, she stunned him.

"The suicide did not take long to fake, and she left the forged confession which she had previously prepared in as prominent a place as she could find. It was not a neat job, not one quarter as neat as her original murder, but *then* she had had ample time to lay her plans—*now* she was working against time.

"Even now, however, the danger was not over. She walked into the lounge and Lady Viola told her of her discovery of Mrs Walton's true identity. By this time Miss Sanctuary was virtually a monomaniac. Anyone who stood between her and her purpose had to be removed. Now it was Lady Viola's turn, and Miss Sanctuary instantly planned as the most likely scene a house in Tooting, which she had already seen the agents about (under her real name) with the object of moving in there when her daughter was married and the trouble had blown over. She invented a fictitious friend who lived there and could give Lady Viola all the information she wanted.

"By this time I also was on her track. Eppoliki told me before he left that he thought her faint after being released from the cupboard was a sham, and I had constructed a hypothesis on the right lines whereby the murders could have been committed by Miss Sanctuary. But, after all, it could have been committed with very much less expenditure of energy by several other people, each with better motives than this inoffensive, good-natured old spinster. When I got Viola's note I still did not realize the connection, and then when I saw from Menzies' photograph that Miss Sanctuary was Mrs Walton's mother, everything clicked into place. The fancied familiarity with Mrs Walton's face was my unconscious interpretation of the family likeness between her and Miss Sanctuary. Here was a plausible motive, and I realized at once that Mrs Mortimer was a figment of the ingenious murderess's fancy, and that Viola's life was in danger." For a moment Charles relived the anxiety of those few minutes. There was a silence in the room. Then a siren hooted on a tug-boat coming up the river; Charles pulled himself together.

"I stole a car that was outside and dashed round. I saw Viola bound, and for a moment I thought I was too late." Charles mopped his forehead. "I wasn't; but I hadn't even the satisfaction of rescuing Viola. When the series of events she had planned came to a head, the old lady found she hadn't the stuff of the killer in her. She couldn't strangle in cold blood a girl who had no evil intentions towards her, and when I broke in they were engaged in making some ridiculous pact of silence…"

The speaker smiled shamefacedly at the Commissioner. "That is why I helped to defeat the ends of justice by giving her the bag in which she had kept a small bottle of poison since she embarked on her carefully planned adventure. That is why I am asking you, when the police evidence is given at the inquest, to make as little use as possible of any evidence that would involve the daughter in publicity."

The Commissioner rubbed his chin meditatively. "You are asking a lot, young man. Gordon's a good coroner, of course, and all the police want is to put in enough evidence to prove that the confession is a real one, and not an act of madness. We shall have to reveal that Miss Sanctuary is really Mrs Church, but we can explain that the motive is a family grudge without particularizing it.

"Look here, young man, you've helped to clear up this case, and I'll go and see the coroner myself and stage-manage the inquest with him."

"Good," said Charles. "I think my personal story in the *Mercury* will set the pace for the rest of the press. Although I sez it that shouldn't, it's a masterpiece of omission, and as I'm an eye-witness, the rest of the press will take it for gospel, and gang warily. Thank the Lord for the law of libel in this country…"

Epilogue

The Garden Hotel was closing at the end of the week. But even if it had been left open till the end of the year, Mrs Walton would still have been methodically packing her clothes, with the slow deliberation of despair.

The door opened. She turned round. In her eyes a faint glimmer of hope flickered and then died.

"Have you come to say good-bye?" she said bravely. "That is very nice of you."

"Come to say good-bye!" exclaimed St Clair Addington. "Why, if I didn't know what a dear little goose you are I should be coming round to demand why you send me the most insulting letter I've ever received in my life."

Mrs Walton sat down abruptly and burst into tears. "Oh, I *had* to say good-bye. Now that everyone knows about my being married and the terrible scandal of it all! It's sweet of you to try and be nice about it, but I knew it was the end. Please—please don't make it worse."

Addington grasped her by the shoulders. "I've a good mind to shake you, Mary," he said. "Oh, I may be a standing joke as an embodiment of conventionality, but I know that now and for ever I would prefer to have you than the patronizing approval of every worthless highfalutin female in London who thinks she's entitled to appraise the reputation of her even Christian. To-morrow we're going to America; somehow or other I shall find Sarto and at Reno divorces are two a penny. I may have to wait a little, but remember I've waited three years already! Then we'll step into my yacht and sail all over the world—to Jamaica once again, and to Peru, and Hawaii and Ceylon, and all the places in the world that must be wonderful if you have someone to share the wonder."

Mrs Walton laughed hysterically. "There doesn't seem much more to say," she said. "Are you always going to be as masterful as this?"

"Worse," answered Addington.

I I

"Viola," said Charles, "I am now the Special Crime Commissioner of the *Mercury* with, I should add, a salary commensurate with the dignity of that office. I feel that I am justified in once again laying my heart at your feet."

"I do wish you would be more serious, Charles," answered Viola fretfully.

"Oh, not quite so serious as that," she said, a moment later. "I can't breathe and you've completely ruined my little hat… Still, I rather like it…"